I0760649

The Invisible Bondage: Emancipate Yourself

The Invisible Bondage: Emancipate Yourself

I'm not afraid of death.
As a matter of fact, I almost invite it.

Devis L. Joseph

I would like to dedicate this book to my mother, Genell M. Joseph, and father, Bruce W. Edwards, who will always be within me as God is. Love you both.

And to all the people who believed in me throughout my journey. Love you all.

Table of Contents

Chapter 1

Necessary

"No, stop! Let me go!" screamed a woman from a distance.

The cry traveled through the thick air and met his ears. It sounded familiar, which made him run even faster through the dark, dense forest. "I'm coming!" he shouted as he made his way to the giant waterfall named The Colossus.

"Brac?" she muttered softly to herself as she recognized the voice. Then she let out a frantic cry. "Go back! It's a trap!"

The boy heard her but didn't listen. He was enraged when he realized it was the voice of his mother, Adore. "Mama!" he said to himself with a whisper of distress and ran even faster. He then approached a wall of clustered vines, covering his face before launching himself through it.

"Artiest!" shouted Brac. "Let her go, you idiot! What the hell is wrong with you?" Brac's hands balled into fists at his side as his chest heaved.

"This is something that has to be done," said Artiest.

Brac lost his patience and charged toward Artiest with a flurry of punches, but Artiest swatted them away as if Brac were a mere gnat.

Artiest collared the scared boy by his ragged shirt, pulled him close, then whispered the same words, "This has to be done," before tossing him down Colossus.

"Brac! No!" shouted his mother, her voice clinging to him as he vanished into the mist of the giant falls.

When his eyes opened, they were quickly blinded by a great illumination. For years, his eyes had witnessed only darkness, but finally, at that moment, he saw light. He came from a dark world engulfed in negativity, so he thought maybe the light was the beginning of something new.

When his eyes began to adapt to the surrounding scene, the first thing they noticed was a beautiful rainbow-filled sky. Brac then blinked, rubbed his eyes, and softly asked himself, "Where am I?" When he rose, he saw lovely autumn-colored trees waving in the wind; there were wildflowers that varied from color to color scattered throughout the thick, fluffy grass. He was utterly confused by what he saw. Looking at his hands, he discovered they were covered with gold rings. His wrist was wrapped with gold bracelets, and around his neck hung a shiny gold chain embedded with a black diamond. He also noticed his clothes and shoes were made of silk. The land looked like heaven, and his attire felt like it belonged to a king.

He wanted to get a better look, so he walked over to a nearby river and gawked at his own reflection. What he saw amazed him. Brac saw a whole new person—he really loved his hair and marveled at the way it was neatly braided into two separate plaits that hung to his shoulders. There were two gold cuffs holding them together with a solid gold crown on top of his head. *Where in the world did I get this stuff?* he wondered. *Only King Vincitor and the people of the castle wear beautiful garments like this. Wait a minute—what if I'm inside the giant castle?* As he considered his reflection, the river revealed an image of him running once more through the dark, dense forest. The forest was called Hofu, the word for fear, and it was fear that gripped him then. "I'm coming!" he shouted.

"Now I remember," he said aloud. "Where is my mother? Where is Artiest? Where am I?"

And then it came. It shone brightly as it hovered over the ground. It was black but still glowed fiercely. He vaguely noticed there was no shadow underneath the dark orb of light. Brac's eyes glimmered with its reflection, and his body felt weightless—he was floating in midair. He reached his hand out to touch it, but it sped away with a swoosh, and he hit the ground.

Chapter 2

The Arial World

It flew around him at an alarming speed, the whooshing sound of the air growing slightly louder. It spun him around in circles as if it was toying with him. He caught his footing and grounded himself, trying to gain focus from the daze it had caused him. Brac relaxed his entire body, closed his eyes, and took a deep breath.

When he opened his eyes, there it was—a ball of light, hovering in midair, close enough for him to touch. It was as though the ball had eyes of its own and was looking at his very soul. It produced a noise like fire blazing and mating with the wind. "What the…" he said, then slowly moved his hand toward it. He was almost there, but *whoosh*! It flew a few feet ahead of him yet again. The light continued to hover slowly over the ground. He followed the ball and was led to a gigantic waterfall. Then it slowly entered, and so did he.

When Brac made it, dripping, to the other side, the ball of light was nowhere to be seen. He had entered a golden cave that looked like it had no end. There were carvings of people growing crops, dancing, fighting, and even one where people were taking flight, stretching all the way down the cave walls into the darkness. Brac took a step farther into the cave but was stopped by a loud growl that echoed off the walls of gold. It paralyzed the boy, and he couldn't even speak. In the darkness, he noticed a pair of eyes locked on him. A black figure moved. As it got closer, its eyes grew. At that very moment, he realized what he was seeing. It was a black-and-gold tiger coming toward him! The boy was still paralyzed by the strong tiger's growl, even though it had stopped seconds before.

"Keynila!" yelled a voice from a distance, and the tiger stopped in its tracks. "Keynila won't harm you," said a beautiful woman who came out of the darkness. She was copper-skinned with bushy, kinky hair and wore a silk-like blouse that hung to her knees. There was also gold all over her body.

"Who are you?" Brac glanced between the woman and the tiger, unsure if he should let his guard down.

She gave him a smirk. "Follow me."

He trailed behind her torchlight through the gold-encrusted cave.

Soon after, it began to get darker until everything around them was pitch black. As they continued to go deeper into the rabbit's hole, Brac noticed his feet were wet. "Where is this water coming from?" he asked.

"This water comes from the beginning of life. It is essential." She reverently paused, anointing herself with the water.

As they exited the cave, the sun rose. They continued to walk; dirt came into view and so did vegetables. The boy saw other people. After more people joined them in the streets, Brac spotted the roofs of huts in the distance. The boy discovered he was in a land that was the complete opposite of his home—his land was dark and gloomy, but the one before him was bright and lively.

"This, Brac," she said proudly, "is the Land of Emancipation!"

It was very alluring. From the ends of his hair to the bottoms of his feet, he felt a tremendous, exquisite sensation—it was the same feeling he'd felt when he'd seen that strange floating black light. "It's…" He grasped for words to describe it. "It's beautiful!" His eyes were captured by the wonders the sun showed. He'd never seen it shine so big, so beautiful, so warm and nurturing. It made him feel vigorous, pliable, incredible—reborn! "What is this feeling?" he asked. "I feel, I feel… great!" In the first world, the sun didn't peek out beyond the clouds—it was cloudy, just like his mind. He'd only ever seen a glimmer from the sun because of the thick clouds that blocked its radiant shine. Picture a world where the sun never shone!

"You feel good after being exposed to things you were once oblivious to, especially the sun." The woman added, "It's your main source of energy."

Brac didn't know a thing about the sun, only that it hid beyond the clouds and was a legend to them all. "The sun?" he questioned. "I've heard about it, but I've never seen it. I've heard of the warmth it brings and the life it sponsors. I guess since we never were truly exposed to it, we never could have felt its warmth."

Grrr. The tiger's growl reverberated through the air, causing Brac's muscles to tense. To his surprise, no one else was startled by the threatening noise.

"What's going on?" He noticed everyone had stopped what they were doing and were looking up to the sky.

"The old man is back." The woman didn't take her eyes off the sky.

Brac squinted against the still unfamiliar sunlight. "Old man? What old man?"

"My father," the woman said bluntly.

"Who is that?" Brac shaded his eyes with his hand, kicking at the dirt in frustration at the vague answers.

The woman turned, and her whole facial expression altered. She looked disgusted at his ignorance. "He's my father!" she proclaimed.

Suddenly, a man appeared out of the rainbow sky.

"What the hell?" asked Brac. "Where did he come from?"

The boy was astounded to see a man appearing out of thin air. The man was a giant. He was very tall, muscular, and looked fierce. And the first person his eyes caught was Brac.

"You must be Brac!" he shouted. "Welcome!" His voice was as deep as an ocean, like the tiger's voice.

His voice paralyzed Brac, but not like Keynila's—more like a god's. "Y-yes, I'm Brac," the boy answered nervously. "Are you… Pah?" he muttered, unable to make eye contact with the man in the sky.

"Pah, that word, you people from the first world and your myths!" The old man nearly spat in derision. "Who is Pah? What does Pah look like? Why do you pray to Pah?" The questions began to pile up.

The boy couldn't answer because he did what everyone else did, and that was obey— obey the rules of Pah or perish. His world was ruled by a wicked man, King Diyar Vincitor. Vincitor was said to receive direct orders from Pah, just as his father had, and his father's father, and so forth.

"You have a lot to learn, my boy, but you will be great!" said the old man. "As long as you are focused, you will prosper. You will learn all of the great secrets that life holds, but you must not rush it. You have all of eternity to receive this knowledge." He paused, then continued, "But take heed, for you will come across many hardships on your journey. Many have traveled on this road you are about to embark, and many have failed. The man who calls himself Vincitor, his great-grandfather was also one of the greats."

The old man sighed, eyelids lowering in disappointment. "He signed a deal with a despicable entity all for power." As he looked up to the sky, he added, "His negativity has swarmed the entire world and all of the people in it. Generation after generation, his family has received this power, and there was no one who dared to stop it."

"But if you're so powerful, why haven't you stopped him?" asked Brac.

"People of our caliber cannot clash. The power unleashed would be too tremendous. The excessive negative and positive energy would be too much for the cosmos to handle. In other words, the dimensions would become unbalanced, and the planets, even the universe, would be destroyed!" he said with a saddened face. "I'm just kidding." He laughed out loud.

"Clown," said the young woman as she leaned over toward Brac.

"We need another savior," the man said. "Everyone is all tied up. Up!" He looked up to the sky and said, "See what I mean? I gotta go, but I'll see you soon, Brac." The man looked at Brac, smiled, then vanished.

"That's his way of answering questions. He'd rather you figure everything out on your own. He normally does not approach newcomers… Well, come on. I have so much to show you," she said.

"Yeah, I'm so confused. I really don't know what to say…" He trailed off then, realizing that, despite having followed her through a dark cave and into a village full of strangers, he still didn't know what to call her. "Wait, what is your name?" he asked.

"My name is Shakoora. I am the only child of the Grand Bilge, who just vanished into thin air."

Bilge was so big and manly, but Shakoora was an untouchable beauty—it was hard to believe the two were related.

"I'm going to first show you around… Where we are now is called the Arial World, a world run by thought. Your world is too, which is why it is so dark and gloomy. The ruler is Vincitor, and his family have been rulers of it for centuries. They are the ones who have engulfed your world with negativity. The mind is a powerful thing—you are soon to learn that." Shakoora continued, "But for now, you must get accustomed to this world and its law."

Brac repeated, “The law?!”

“Yes, even in the other world there are laws, but the laws here are different. We go by Universal Law,” Shakoora explained. “The law of the universe is the only one a thing should follow. Nothing more or nothing less. If anything has too many rules to follow, then it will become a slave, and the mind will be contained. The laws that are supposed to be followed come naturally with instinct, such as birth, hunger, or thirst. If you were to stub your toe on that rock, you would react without thinking. Our rules are not rules. Instead, they follow the natural law of instinct.” She gave Brac a condescending smile. “When you begin to understand, you will perceive everything on a higher level.”

The first place they arrived was a well-put-together shack. It was smothered in flowers, and all sorts of animals ran around it. The animals brushed against Shakoora as if she were a mother returning home to her children.

“You see, animals do not run from us here—they embrace us. Now, hold your finger out,” she ordered.

The animals quickly scattered when he followed the woman’s request.

“You see, they run from you because they can sense your fear, and they know that when a thing has fear, it can be dangerous. Close your eyes, and clear your mind. Know the power is coming to you. Believe it. That will attract it,” she said.

However, while Brac’s eyes were closed, he heard a woman screaming, “No! Stop! Let me go!” At the sound of the scream, all of the animals scattered yet again.

“What just happened?” asked Shakoora.

“I—I just saw my mother.” He wept. “She was on the edge of Colossus. Do you know if she’s still alive?”

Shakoora looked at him, then turned away. “Come,” she said. “There is someone you should meet.”

Chapter 3

Femme de Tunne

"Mama!" shouted Shakoora over the squeaking and creaking of the door.

"Huh?!" answered an elderly voice. "I'm in the kitchen! Bring your friend back here!"

Brac looked at Shakoora and asked, "How does she know that I'm with you?"

"Umph… she's no first world woman, ya know. Mom, hey, this is Brac!"

Her mother cut in. "I knew Brac before he knew himself," she said with a smile. "How was everything in the first world before you left?"

"How could you know me before I knew myself? Where am I?" he said. "I remember that it was nothing like this! This world is magnificent. I have seen things here that in the first world would kill you. For example, when I first saw Keynila, I was paralyzed by her growl. I had no idea she wasn't a killer!"

Shakoora's mother laughed. "Keynila eats fruits and vegetables. You see, the food here is very filling." She added, "If you were to eat an apple, you would be full for some time. The soil here is a hundred times more potent than the soil in the first world. Remember, this dimension is heightened. The gravity is also different. Haven't you noticed?"

"Well, come to think of it, I actually do feel kind of heavy," Brac responded.

The elderly lady said, "I know you never tasted freedom before. Shucks, you all have been in bondage for a very long time. The only ones who tasted freedom were the Great Elders, but even they were defeated by the Vincitors. Their power exceeded the elders' because of their ruthlessness, anger, and drive to conquer. The Great Elders are still very powerful, of course, but we'll need some new recruits if we ever want to banish the Vincitors."

"New recruits? Mom, I could have been a recruit, and you expect a first world person to be one? I've been here all my life!" Shakoora stormed out of the room.

"She'll be all right," said the elder woman. "Now, Brac, you will be going on a grand adventure." She added, "I can't wait to see how you evolve… This is so exciting!"

"A recruit, like in an army? Oh, and can I get your name? Everything's been moving so fast that I even forgot to ask Shakoora her name when we met," he said.

"My name!" she said with great dignity. "My name is Femme de Tunne, and yes, like an army. When we get our army together, Vincitor will be defeated. I'm sure of it! But we need your help, Brac!" she exclaimed. "I've been watching you, and we can tell you will be a great warrior!"

But all of a sudden, it was too much for Brac to handle. His mouth had gone dry, and he couldn't respond. How could he react to something so vast? He had fought before—plenty of times—but going through all of those changes made his head spin.

"The lazy bums who refuse to train and become great warriors stay here. They might make sorry recruits, but they're good helpers," she continued. "As you can see, it is rather perfect here… but they have to live an eternity knowing that they did not go back, and all they can do is praise the ones who did become gods, like myself! It's not that they did not have the ability to endure the training, but they just took the easy route, so to say. Some just wanted peace. They occupy themselves with gardening, sitting in the shade—things old, washed-up people do. I wouldn't dare! I'd go crazy!"

"Mother," said Shakoora as she barged back in, "that's no way to talk! Everyone here is loyal to this world. They just wanted some peace and quiet." She turned to Brac. "I would love to go out there into the lower dimension, but my parents won't allow it because they say it's too dangerous for me." She huffed. "I'm one of the most powerful beings in the universe! I can handle my own weight. I've only heard about what goes on in your world, Brac, but I'm dying to see it in real life. I want to know how it is away from here."

"Your father is overprotective of you, but I feel like you should experience the first world. It would help expand your horizons, just like this world will do for Brac. You both know things the other does not, so you can really learn from one another," Shakoora's mother muttered. "Who knows what else will happen? Maybe I'll get those grandchildren I've been longing for."

"Mama!" shouted Shakoora. "I heard that! I'm a warrior, not a breeder! And why do you want grandchildren so badly? I can't be out of training for a month!"

"But I thought it took nine months for a baby to be born," Brac said cluelessly.

"Can't you just hush! Didn't we tell you that this is a whole other dimension?!" Shakoora shouted.

"Don't talk to him like that. He's a savior," said Tunne. "He might save your a—"

But before she could get her words out, it came back.

Chapter 4

The Void

It was the light! But the only person who seemed surprised was Brac. "That's the same light that led me here!"

Tunne laughed. "You mean, you led yourself here, my boy?" The elderly woman added, "You have a lot to learn. Learning is the main road to truth. This light represents your true inner being. The stronger it is, the more powerful your clair gets."

"Clair," repeated Brac. "What is a clair?"

The light zoomed toward Brac and hovered in front of his face as if it were looking back at him. He finally built the courage to try to touch it once again. Brac's outstretched hand got closer and closer to the light, which inched nearer in response. Then, without warning, it flew into his fingers, and both Brac and the light disappeared.

"Hmph… He didn't even get a chance to eat his food!" said Tunne.

"I hope he can handle it," said Shakoora with a hint of worry.

"Well," Tunne muttered. "Maybe you should go make sure he's okay. You've been there before."

"What are you expecting from this, Ma?" said Shakoora.

"Oh nothing, I just want to make sure the boy's fine. He is a savior, you know."

Shakoora responded, "Yeah, I bet." Worry dragged down those words.

***

They went through dimension after dimension as they flew through the bowels of time. Any questions in his mind melted away, and all he could do was watch as time faded away. Coming to a realization, he asked, “Where am I?” while regaining his sense of self, then quickly raised his voice. “Hello, is anybody here?”

As he waited for a response, he thought his feet touched solid ground. The feeling was abruptly ripped away; he began to panic, and as his mind became discombobulated, he started to fall. Brac screamed at the top of his lungs. His body came to a halt, whiplash cracking his neck. He hung suspended in the darkness above a raging ocean. Whatever force was playing with him didn’t let him rest for long. His lungs tightened as he fell into the depths of the ocean. He realized he couldn’t do it anymore. Desperate for a breath, he opened his mouth and took the deepest one he possibly could. Rather than suffocating ocean water, fresh air filled his lungs.

As soon as he realized he had inhaled air and not water, the ocean dried up, and he stood instead on solid ground. Everything was still dark.

As he put his arms out to feel for anything around him, a mysterious glow lit up ahead. It looked as if it was dancing and moving closer to him. As it grew nearer, it reached out to engulf him. It was fire. He had a flashback of the terror it had caused—people screaming at the top of their lungs, bodies being burned—and his mind was in the midst of the horrific scenery.

So, he did what any typical person would have done—he flew into a panic. He jumped up and down and ran in circles, terrified. As he swatted at the flames, he found no burns on his fingertips. At a second glance, his clothing was untouched. The fire crackled merrily along his arms, but he was entirely uninjured. It wasn’t even hot.

“What’s going on?” he asked. “First the water, and now this. All the things that I know can kill me… they aren’t even harming me! In this place, am I dead or something?” As he began to analyze the nothingness, he thought, *If all this is real, then I have no choice*. Immediately after the realization, he closed his eyes and took a deep breath.

Behind his eyelids, he saw her just the way she had looked in the first world. “Mama!” he murmured.

Her back still turned to him, she said, “The food’s ready!”

“Mama, I—I was lost. I was scared.”

Everything started to fade as he reached out to his mother. She began to move farther and farther away. “Mama, wait, come back!” he shouted as it grew pitch black.

“You defy me, boy!” called a heavy voice from the darkness. “Now die!” It was Diyar Vincitor. He towered over Brac with his devilish looks, a gray-faced, red-eyed demon!

He had a nerve-racking tone, and Brac fell even farther into the abyss.

Chapter 5

The Beginning

He landed yet again in the midst of darkness. Before he could feel anything other than the terror that Vincitor's presence had caused, he heard a loud cry. It was piercing, like an infant's, but he couldn't see where it was coming from. He could hear other people, but he couldn't put their words together. Between the crying and the people blabbering, his head spun in circles.

"Hand me the blade," came a voice in the distance.

"Here," said another.

Brac tried to grasp what was going on, but he could not see a thing.

Orbs in all colors of the rainbow floated around him, strikingly similar to the light that had brought him there.

Brac realized he was in the middle of a birth.

"What is going on?" he asked. "Hey, ma'am! Sir!" Brac tried to reach out to anyone who would listen. But coming to the realization that no one could hear him, he stopped.

Then, from a distance, he heard a baby screaming. He began to go toward it. When he made it to the bed, his breath caught his chest. It was his mother! "Ma!" He hesitated and took a step back in disbelief. *Mama... she looks so different. So much younger. What's going on?*

There was no sign of grief or shame on her face. She looked happy. She wore her hair down to her shoulders with a beautiful black silk gown and a gold chain embedded with multicolored jewels. She was just as beautiful as the gemstones. What stood out was her deep-brown skin, her dreamy eyes, and her gorgeous smile. She also had long coal-black hair like a goddess. Why, he knew it was his mother, but not the one he actually knew. She had been through horrible things in the first world, but there, wherever he was, she looked stupendous!

"Brac, look at him," she said softly.

"My boy," said a voice.

"He said his boy!" shouted Brac. "So that must mean he's my—my father!" Brac looked at his dad for the first time, noticing light-brown eyes and tanned skin that matched his own. "Wow, he may really be my father, but I was told my father was a wayfarer, and he left as soon as my mother became pregnant with me. And I know that look. That's the look of a warrior."

"My love," stated Brac's father.

"Yes?" answered Adore.

"What will you name him?" he asked.

"No need to ask," she responded. The couple looked lovingly at the baby, but Adore's features soon began to crumple. "I mean, I have fallen in love with a rebel and have blossomed his seed. My father does not approve of me running away. He will send Artiest to come and—"

"Enough," he said soothingly. "Your father is the least of my worries, but I will say that he is a part of them. But I won't let this moment be ruined by problems I can solve afterward. If Artiest comes, he comes," he declared. "Now, let me hold my son."

Adore's momentary hesitation gave way under the affectionate look Brac's father gave her. "Here, watch his head."

When Brac the elder held the baby, Brac saw a slow smile stretch across his face. "My family and my people are all I have. I promise I will do anything to protect them. I swear on my ancestors!" He wept, then smiled.

All of a sudden, his entire demeanor changed. "Here, my love, take him and don't come out. I have a matter to settle." He then kissed Adore on the lips and walked through the crowd. Before leaving, he looked around at everyone, nodded his head, smiled, and walked out.

"I know you're here. Show yourself," he said. Movement came from the forest, and Artiest appeared.

"You knew I was here," said Artiest.

"Yes, I felt your presence when you first appeared. I just was savoring the moment with my family," Brac Sr. said. "Well, you ready?"

"You know I am," Artiest replied with a menacing look to back it up.

Back inside, the boy was in shock. "It can't be. No no no." He shook his head. "This is crazy! Who would want to kill my father just for being with my mother?" he said.

A voice whispered from behind him, "Vincitor!"

He looked back quickly, and there was a pitch-black figure wearing a large gold medallion with diamonds that shone like a rainbow. The figure had teeth as white as clouds, white tiger skin covering his torso, and plaited hair hanging to his feet. He had a glow that came from his space-colored skin. It was an aura like no other. It was so strong that Brac's father and Artiest felt it.

"What is that?" asked Artiest.

"I don't know," said Brac Sr., "but that power damn near swept us under the rug!"

"Sometimes I like to let people know what type of power darkness holds!" the pitch-black figure replied with a smooth, deep voice that shook Brac. "I am what is, and I am what will be. I am infinite and definite. I am the present moment, and the far-flung future! I am everything!"

Even Brac's father and Artiest were shaken by that tremendous strength. "I guess that this means this is our final showdown," said Brac Sr.

"Just to let you know, before I kill you, you are a very worthy opponent." Artiest showed great respect.

Brac Sr. charged. *"Ahhh!"* His war cry rang out through the air, and he leaped so hard off the ground that he left a pothole-sized crater in it.

"Come on," Artiest snarled.

"I'll wear your skull as a sign of respect!" Brac Sr. shouted.

The two men then began to brawl. The impact of every blow made the vicinity tremble, and the onlookers watched in awe as they hid from the battling men. Neither of the men spoke. They only grunted in pain or with effort as their bones popped and muscles tore.

"Well," said the strange man. "They fight for nearly half the day, and I already know who winds up victorious, so there's no point in watching it all."

"Half the day?" questioned Brac. "But that's impossible! How could someone last that long in a fight? It's like a mini war. I can hear their bones popping and snapping!"

The man answered, "You see, they are on the level of people of the second world. They can heal themselves and continue to battle. But," he stated, "they can still lose energy and pass out. Passing out is good, though, because that is sleep, and sleep is really deep meditation. This is one truth I'll teach you now. The others will come in time."

"What is meditation?" asked Brac.

"Meditation is the complete focus on nothing. Nothing is defined as the void, emptiness, darkness. It is where things are created. If you meditate and train daily, you can become the master of your mind, body, and spirit," he explained.

Brac was utterly confused. He had no idea what the stranger was talking about. Suddenly, a booming sound came from right under them. It was Artiest. Brac's father had smashed his face into the ground, attempting to crush his skull beneath his boot.

Brac Sr. stomped relentlessly. When he stopped and caught his breath, he said, "I told you. Now, I'm tired of being labeled as a menace. It's time to end this!"

But as he walked away, Artiest began to move. He pulled his face from the ground. "I'm… not… dead yet," he growled as he struggled to get to his feet. "It's not over until one of us is sent to another dimension or both of us die from fatigue! I will give you my everything! This is not just a battle of men," he shouted, "but a battle of *gods*!"

"Artiest, you will die today. I promise you that!"

Again, they charged right back into one another.

It was the most intense thing Brac had ever witnessed. "Why are they fighting like this?" he asked.

"They are great warriors, Brac. Your father wants to prove to the world that he isn't disobeying Pah's laws. The god you know as Diyar Vincitor claims to be the only god. His father was the same way, and his father's father also."

Brac found himself puzzled. "But King Vincitor is very strong. I've seen him kill many, he—"

"That's enough!" the strange man shouted. "You know nothing yet about true strength. You have not even been in battle. Those lousy fistfights you have been in mean nothing. You saw what Artiest did to you, huh? Now, shut up!"

Brac said not another word.

"Your father wants to save humanity from deception. He is very strong."

Brac remained silent.

"Artiest is out for knowledge and power. But the rest is left to you to find out," he explained without turning away from the fight.

The strange man's refusal to look Brac's way left him no other option than to pay attention to the battle before them. "They are really fighting," Brac said.

"I know they are!" the strange man snapped.

They watched the rest of the brawl in silence.

Chapter 6

The End of a Long Battle
And the Beginning of a Long Journey

They fought and fought until the end of one's time. "Artiest!" said Brac Sr. "This is the end of the road… It is time!"

When Brac Sr. said that, Artiest smiled and charged at him. However, Brac Sr. just stood there as if he were helpless. "I'm tired of fighting now…" And off with his head.

Artiest picked it up slowly. "I respect you," he mumbled to the decapitated head. But no one else respected Artiest. All of the people started to crawl out of hiding and charge toward him.

Before the civilians could reach him, a deep voice boomed, "Artiest!" The sound of it was so fierce that the people cringed.

Then, everyone stopped in the middle of their rampage. When they all looked back, their jaws dropped along with their hearts. It was him!

"Diyar Vincitor," Brac whispered, the words shaky.

He was outfitted in gold-and-black-striped armor from head to toe. His eyes were blood red, and his sclerae were black as night. He wore his coal-black hair in a long ponytail. His appearance was fearsome alone, but an aura of power surrounded him that would make the bravest man quake. No smile, no horse, no men. *Why is he here?*

That was the only thing people could think—they were too frightened to even mumble.

"King Diyar, I have completed the mission… sir."

Vincitor just stood there. "Don't you feel it?" he asked. "That presence."

That's when Brac looked at the strange man. "What? He knows we are here?" He trembled with fear.

"We felt that same thing in the middle of our battle, but I no longer can be sure if it is still here," said Artiest.

"Oh, how weak you are, Artiest," said Vincitor.

Artiest clenched his jaws and gritted his teeth. "Hmph." He gestured at the decapitated body.

"Off with his head, huh? The old-fashioned way. Well, at least you have a trophy. You'll gain no strength fighting a thrall." Vincitor burst out laughing.

"I'm gone," Artiest muttered. "I won't be back for some time… I have something I must do."

"Well, since you've decapitated our friend here, I have no more missions for you to complete," Vincitor concluded.

"I have no one else to fight; I've slaughtered all of the people that you've asked, and he was the strongest of all."

Vincitor answered, "The only reason I came was because of that massive energy I felt. It was too good to pass by, but now I don't even sense it. So I guess I'll be gone now. The gods are indeed watching. You two must have been putting up a damn good fight… or maybe it was here for something else." With that, Vincitor turned his back on the scene and slowly vanished into the dense wilderness.

"Bury that body," said Artiest as he waved his hand dismissively at the townspeople. "You all may want to visit it." Then he did the strangest thing: he looked back directly at Brac, then at the hut where he and his mother lay.

"Did he just… see us?" asked Brac.

"Hmph, maybe," said the man.

"But I thought no one could," he said. "The people in the hut, my mother, none of them could see us. And he didn't notice us before. Why now?"

"Someone like Artiest is very different."

"Different? Different how?"

"Come, it's time to go."

Brac was tired of his questions not being answered. "Why don't you answer me?" he shouted. "You're beginning to piss me off!" He was furious. "All of this crap," he cried out. "I don't understand. Why am I here? What is the point of me seeing these things if I can't freaking understand!? Huh? I just want to go back home!" First his mother, then his father? The losses were piling up on his shoulders. "Take me back! I'm not ready for this! Take me home! I'm not ready!" With a scream, he fell to his knees and pounded the ground, repeatedly shouting, "Screw this!" He began to sob. "I just want to go home!"

Brac was so out of it he didn't even notice he had pounded a giant crater into the ground.

"Look at your strength, boy," the strange man said. "You are one of the chosen few who can change things, and you're sitting here crying like a lost cub. If you listen to us, then we'll change your eternity. Just believe! That is all. Do you want to go back to being a thrall, a simple slave? You must free yourself from this invisible bondage. If you don't, then you'll never reach your true potential!"

Those words touched Brac so much that he summoned enough strength to rise after the outburst of power he had used. He definitely was not used to it, so it took more willpower for him to get to his feet than just his physical strength.

"The power of belief helps everything grow. You will learn the ways of the universe," the stranger proclaimed. "You will hold the power of a god in your hands. Your training begins *now*!" Then they vanished.

Chapter 7

A Mother's Pain

Her eyes flickered as she slowly began to wake, her vision blurry and her body glued to her bed. "What… what happened?" she asked.

"Adore, you passed out after giving birth," said Ami, the woman who nursed her.

"Where is…" It took her a moment to form the question, but it came out clearly once she had. "Where is… Brac?"

"Over there, he's asleep. He's been out also."

Adore looked over to her son. "Where is his father?" she asked.

"We—well," Ami said hesitantly, "he went outside."

"Well, could you please tell him that I said to come?"

"Well, um… I can't lie to you, Adore."

"What do you mean? Is Brac in some sort of trouble?" she asked warily.

"You see, Artiest came, and they were fighting—Artiest killed Brac, Adore!" she shouted. "We all saw the whole thing." Her voice dropped to a whimper. "We are all cowards—we should have helped him!"

"It's okay, Ami. Those two are on a completely different level than the rest of us; no one could have done a thing but sacrifice their life trying."

"And your father came also," said Ami while staring at the ground.

"And what did he do?"

"Well, he showed up after the fact. He talked about a power, a very strong power."

"Hmm, I think I know what power he was talking about…" she said. "Grab Brac for me. I'll need you to hold him. We have to say our goodbyes." She began to struggle to get out of the bed, grunting and using all she had.

"Adore, you should not be—"

"I'm okay!" shouted Adore. "Sorry for yelling, but it is the time to be strong, not merciful. My father will be back, and you know for whom: my son. I felt his power—it was something like I have never felt before. It gave me a strange feeling. I don't know what we're going to do, but I'll tell you what: from now on, we all have to train harder—no one will be considered weak! We all have to start fighting back!" she said. "And since Brac is gone, we're on our own. Get ready because it is going to be a wild ride from here on out."

As Adore and Ami, who was carrying Brac, made their way to the body, no one made a sound. The hole was already dug, and people were mourning, glancing at them then putting their heads down.

"No need to mourn, my people!" said Adore. "This is the time where we all become what Brac was and in the pages of history always will be. And that, my people, is strong! No heads down! From now on, we will keep our heads to the sky, and we will make a brighter day. The sun will shine again. My father, who is a *despicable* man, will bow down and kiss the ground we walk on! My people, I promise we will see better days."

She stared at Brac's headless body and said, "I love you and will carry on your glory until the day I meet the same dirt. We will not lose another soul to Vincitor or any other kingdom that crosses us. We will break down and rebuild. We will form an alliance among ourselves. No one will ever take us as weak again." Her voice was strong and fierce. The people were astounded by her bravery. But on the inside, she was in atrocious pain.

Chapter 8

Uncle Dev

The stranger grabbed Brac's shoulder, and they were jerked back into the darkness, flying through the dimensions silently. Tears ran down Brac's face as he thought of his father's death, and his thoughts were overtaken by a strong desire to get revenge against Artiest.

"My name is Noir," the stranger finally said. "I am the god of time and travel. I will introduce you to everything you will need to know to get to the next level. It is your time, Brac."

At that moment, their feet touched the ground. Brac regained his footing before asking, "Why now?"

"Well, it was time for you to learn the truth about your family's past. So much has gone on in the last century, and you are blind to it all. It is time for your eyes to be opened. What you just witnessed back there, that was a part of your rebirth; you will never be the same again."

Unable to argue, Brac only stared at him.

"Now, if I had just sent you back in time alone, you would have been out of your mind. You don't know how to control your emotions; they are your strength. You have a power deep inside of you that can either be good or bad."

Brac still could not believe what Noir was saying.

"When people cross over, they learn what many cannot learn from the first world. There are only a few who decided to go back. Vincitor was one of them, but something made him turn into the despicable man he is today. He abused the powers of the universe and manipulated your world. He is so powerful that his negativity screwed up the realm, which is why the sun doesn't shine."

Brac was just happy he was finally getting some answers. "Okay, so where are we going now?" he asked.

"We're going to meet one of your ancestors. His name is Dev. He is your uncle."

Brac had never met any other family members besides his mother. "So, is he strong?"

"Very," Noir answered with a smirk.

When they got to their destination, it was the weirdest place Brac had ever seen. There were giant suns all over the gorgeous purple-pink sky and huge gold gargoyles flew around them. Massive caves were lit up with emeralds, rubies, and diamonds. People were walking around drinking out of huge mugs and bottles, laughing, joking, and dancing to music. The music itself was coming from the sky. The trees were full of various fruits, and there were giant gardens everywhere full of life. It was a whole new world and very strange indeed.

Then, there was a loud sound. It was a grumbling, deeper than the tiger's, and it rang through the air. A big white contraption flew through the sky, a large seat up front with a flat back. A beep pierced Brac's eardrums as a person in in the front smacked the wheel.

"What is that?" asked Brac.

Noir just shook his head. "That is your crazy uncle. He's just full right now," he said.

Brac looked at him and asked, "Full? You mean like food?"

"No, liquid melas. It is what makes us strong, but too much can make you drunk. It's like power in a cup. It's made from dark fruits and other dark matter. It makes everything inside and outside the body stronger, but it takes a lot of mental stability to handle the potency of melas. We are all born with an amount we can handle. Your uncle is a very strong individual."

"Hey there!" yelled Dev as he pulled up—well, landed—in the old white contraption, which creaked and squeaked and wheezed out black smoke. "Hey fellas!" He had a high-pitched voice and wore a black silk shirt, silk pants, two huge gold ankle bracelets, a gold chain with a giant black diamond, and no shoes. "Noir!" he said. "How ya been?" He had a very strong French Creole accent.

"I've been busy working," he said.

"As usual. You're always on the move. And you," he said, turning to Brac, "you look familiar." He got in Brac's face. "Hmmm, those features. You look like…" He peered deeply into Brac's eyes while rubbing his chin. "You look just like my baby brother! Yep!"

"Why, he is your great-nephew, you know. He is the grandson of Diyar Vincitor and Docente Guider," Noir said.

"Hmm. What a screwed-up bloodline," he said. "How did that happen? Those families are like oil and water." Without waiting for an answer, he continued. "Well, I guess it is what it is," he said. "Now, may I ask what you are here for?"

Brac looked at Dev, then Noir. "Um, I—"

"He is here for your tutoring, sir," Noir slid in. "He needs to learn from his ancestors. You all can—"

"I don't do the babysitting thing," said Dev. "I don't have time; I'm too busy creating. And it's not like he'll be the one!"

Noir gave him a severe look. "That's why we're here, but he needs you more than any of us. He needs your guidance. You are the catalyst to his perfection. You ran away from your family and created this great world and everything in it to make yourself happy."

Dev looked around, then looked at Noir. "You know, everything you are saying is true. I did leave… but I had to. I needed some freedom from the ways my siblings and parents ran things." His face relaxed, and a smile came as he said, "I became my own man by doing that, and no one has ever given my creations a good compliment."

"Well, you've never given them a chance," said Noir. "Brac, what do you think about your uncle's creations?"

Brac looked at Noir, then his uncle. "Well," he said. "I think"—he looked his uncle in the eyes—"I think they're tight!"

"Hmph, so you want to learn how to create, huh?" Dev said proudly.

"Well, yes!" Brac answered.

"Well, I'll let you in on a secret: it will be one of the most difficult things you will ever learn. I will train you in the art of creation. But!" he cautioned. "Know you can get lost in the Void—and before you ask, the Void is nothingness, blackness—and you have to understand, this will be very, very difficult and frightening."

"Well, it cannot get any worse than where I'm from."

When Brac said that, his uncle gave him a very disgusted stare. "Where you're from!" he muttered. "The first world was born from the Void, but it is not nearly as terrible. Trying to compare the two shows how little you know. From now on, don't try to talk about things you don't understand. The way you think in the Void is the way you live. Think of something too long and hard, and it will begin to manifest. Before you even go, you will need some proper training. As soon as the music starts, you rise, and you will not rest until it stops. Now, go get some rest," he said. "Noir, I have this. I will let you know when he is ready."

Noir looked at Dev, and then at Brac, nodded his head, tapped his staff on the ground, and vanished.

"I will get a gnorl to show you to your resting place." Dev made a loud screeching noise that sounded like an eagle. And out of the sky came a giant golden bird-like creature. It was beautiful but fierce looking, pure gold with eyes like twin abysses.

"What in all death is that?" shouted Brac.

"This is one of my greatest creations. He is a gnorl. He can spot anything his rider wants him to and go anywhere. And he is indestructible… Well, damn near."

The giant creature just stood there, staring at Brac with its pitch-black eyes. Then, it screeched. Its voice was loud and powerful enough to shake the surrounding area.

"All right, neph, get on."

Brac gave his uncle a how-in-the-hell-do-I-do-that type of look.

"His wings, idiot," Dev muttered.

"Hey, you're going to have to stop calling me that!" Brac shouted. "I have never ridden a creature before, especially not something as gigantic as this."

Brac eyed the beast hesitantly before saying, "Well, here goes." He began to climb up the giant creature's wing, and all of a sudden, it tossed him aboard. He landed right on his bottom. "Ah! Hey, hey, hey!" he shouted as the creature flapped its wings.

"You will be fine! The gnorl knows exactly what he's doing!"

Before Brac could ask what that meant, the gnorl took off toward the rainbow sky.

Chapter 9

Bird's-Eye View

Flying through the beautiful sky and breathing in the delicious air filled Brac with a joy he'd never experienced. There was no ash from volcanoes, no smoke from fires, no reek of decaying bodies—just fresh, clean air. Brac's body felt light. His eyes were closed, but he couldn't hide his wide smile. "This is amazing!" he said softly. Opening his eyes, he found he could see the whole planet. The gnorl had flown them into the stars. "It's beautiful..." he whispered. "Why, I've never seen anything like it." The view was breathtaking—the planet looked like a giant ball of rainbow ice cream. "Can I see more?" he asked.

"Well, sure!" came a suave deep voice.

"Wha—" Before Brac could get his words out, the gnorl sped off like a rocket. "You can talk?" Brac shouted over the rush of wind.

"I can do many things," answered the creature.

"I didn't know you could talk!"

"Well, now you do, Brac," he said.

When they made it back, the gnorl stopped in midair. "So, what do you want to do next? You have a big day when the third sun comes around, so you might as well enjoy."

"Well, first off, do you have a name?" Brac asked.

"Well… the only name I will have is the one you give me. You are my rider, and that's the only way I can talk to anyone. They have to ride and enjoy, and you did just that."

"So, what about 'Gnorl'?"

"No, that is the name of my species. I would like a personal one," he said. "Every rider I have ever had ended up creating their own creations and planets, so I am nameless."

Brac sat there for a while. "I've never given anything its own name before, but I can give it a try…" He thought and thought until—"Hey, I've got it: Suave!"

"Suave?" the creature repeated.

"Yeah, it means charming, elegant, confident. You have a very smooth, deep voice, and the way you fly is so elegant, and you seem confident, so the name fits you perfectly."

"Hm, it sounds good. I like it!" he shouted.

"Ha! Now let's go, Suave. Show me the beauty of this world!"

"You got it!"

They cruised through the air, dropping lower and lower. People were walking, planting, cooking, drinking, and dancing as they flew by.

"It's really calming to see this—all these people living in abundance and harmony together—isn't it, Brac?" asked Suave.

"It really is. We couldn't do this in my world because they'd try to slaughter us both, but the people here aren't even paying attention."

Some kids ran along behind Suave and Brac, and others just pointed at them.

"No one here will do any harm," said Suave. "This is a world of peace. You'll never be the same after you leave here."

"Buddy, I'm not even the same now," he said.

"Well, I have something to show you," said Suave. He flew past everyone and into a giant cave lit up with orbs of light.

"Hey, those look like the light I saw when I first opened my eyes," Brac marveled.

"Well, they are, but they have lives of their own, you know. They travel through dimensions too, and they help guide people. When a person becomes truly free, they can live within them. That's the quality that gives people power—freedom!"

Upon reaching the end of the cave, they passed through a giant waterfall that led them to a huge lake. The water was so clear that you could see all the way to the bottom. Fish swam over the gold and emeralds covering the bottom of the lake. The jewels sparkled and shone in the sunlight, reflecting off Suave's entire body and glistening off Brac's eyes.

"This is so pretty," said Brac. "What is this place?"

"Why, this is Belleza, the place of beauty. It's the most beautiful place on this planet."

To Brac's delight, even the trees seemed to shine, and the area had its own sun.

"That is the second sun, so where is the first one?" asked Brac.

"Well, it's a long way down, so you'll see it eventually. The third sun shines on us. I had to travel through a dimension just to get through that tunnel. This world is very different from your own, for it holds so much more power. This part of the universe is very, very distinctive. No one knows the *true* essence of life, Brac," he said, and concluded, "We only think we know."

"But I never recognized when you did it. When Noir traveled I felt, well, different," he said.

"Ha, that's because I travel differently, way faster than Noir," he said. "You'll be sleeping here tonight."

"Okay, but how am I going to get back?" Brac asked. "You said that tunnel was hundreds of miles, maybe even thousands! How am I supposed to go home? Walk? Run?" Brac's voice cracked with fear. "You can't just leave me here!"

"You have many great qualities that are hidden deep within you, and learning to use them is your first task." They landed, entering the beautiful forest that surrounded the lake. "This is where you will stay until you find your way. You must not worry. It is very easy for creations to be made here. Fear is your worst enemy, Brac," he said, staring him right in the eyes, which creeped Brac out even more. "Now I will be leaving."

Brac cowered. "But what am I supposed to do? I don't know anything about this place." His eyes got teary.

"Coming from where you're from, this should not bother you. Goodbye, Brac." He flew into the sky and vanished, leaving Brac looking like a lost child.

Chapter 10

Finding a Way

He stood there for a while, still staring at the sky to make sure it was real. "He'll be back! I'm the savior, so he has no choice!" he said, trying to project a confidence he didn't feel. "I know he will…" Brac was afraid.

"Sometimes you have to save yourself," came the small voice of a child.

But from where?

Brac looked up and down in a panic. "Who said that?" he asked, shocked.

"Shhh… quiet. Your fear will attract the worst. You must not do anything to draw them here, or anywhere else," said the mysterious voice.

"Just tell me who you are. I can't help but panic! Talking to a strange voice is pretty creepy! I'm not used to anything like this. I'm used to seeing who and where voices come from."

Then it grew silent.

"Hello, are you still there?" But he got no answer. Suddenly, the ground began to tremble, and Brac fell. "What's going on?" he shouted as the ground began to crack and started to rise like something was pushing its way out from beneath it.

"Here I go!"

Right before his eyes stood a giant tree. It had shot out of the ground so quickly, but it had to be at least two hundred feet, if not taller.

"I will show you my strongest and most knowledgeable form," it said. It shone a bright-red color and was wide enough that Brac thought he could comfortably fit inside it thirty times over. "You should not fear me. I am the knowledge of life." As it spoke, its voice grew deeper. "I am what you thought and what you still think. I am what you fear"—and the voice faded somewhat—"but fear should not exist." The first voice returned, that of a child, soft and innocent. "Fear is the thing that makes you weak. Why worry when everything you see, hear, and touch are the same thing—just some more contained than others. Take, for instance, the sun. It is bursting with energy, and you are too, but your energy is contained. You have to learn how to use it, Brac."

Why, the voice was that of an intelligent being. "Listen," said Brac, "I don't know about anything that is going on. I'm completely lost."

"Well, Brac, you're talking to the right person."

He could not distinguish whether the voice was that of a young boy or a young girl.

"My name is Arbre. I was once a lost child, and I was killed by fear," said the voice.

Brac realized that it was the voice of a girl. "You're a… a girl?" he asked.

"Yes, I certainly am," she said. "I was killed because fear froze my body. I'm trapped in the form of the thing that killed me."

"A tree? How did a tree kill you?"

"Well you see, the fruits that the tree carried were very, very high up—even the lowest branch was probably sixty feet tall. But they were some of the most delicious fruits on our planet. The fruit of that tree gave power to those who ate them. So, I climbed up the tree and grabbed as many as I could. I was still quite hungry, and the next one I saw was the biggest one yet. I should have been more mindful of the color of the mighty fruit. They were mostly white, but this one was black—those are the most potent ones. I grabbed it and took a bite, then all of a sudden, my body glowed with a strange dark aura. I panicked and fell, but I don't remember hitting the ground. When I awoke, I was here. I don't know if I went through a dimension or if I died. But I don't think I'm dead. I mean, I don't *feel* dead."

"Well," said Brac, "I certainly don't know too many—" He paused. "Well, I don't know *anyone* that can turn into a tree."

"You see, on my planet, things are very different. To make a long story short, it is a very rare and mysterious place. Dinosaurs still exist, and magic is heavy. When I woke up, I had nobody. I could no longer feel the magic of my planet, and when I looked in the lake, I saw nothing," she whimpered.

"I mean, I didn't see you either," said Brac. "All I heard was your voice and then *boom*! I'm talking to a giant tree."

"Since I've been here, strange things have been happening. I don't know who I am most of the time. My identity turns into a blur. My mind is just raging with knowledge, but I can't put it all together," she said with worry. "I don't know what to do."

As Brac pondered on what life would be like as a tree, something told him to look up, and when he did, he saw a strange glow.

Chapter 11

Finding a Way Out

"Arbre!" Brac shouted. "Something is glowing up there."

Arbre was quiet for a while. "It's the fruit!" she said. "One has bloomed! I can feel it, Brac, I can feel it!"

"So, can't you just bring it down or make it fall or something?" Brac asked.

"I don't have that much control yet. I can only sprout from a seed to this form," she said.

"Well, I actually think if I eat that fruit, we both can get out of here. It's just a wild guess. You say you don't know if you're dead or just went through a dimension, right?"

"Yes. I really don't know. I think it's fear, but then again, maybe something else happened," said Arbre.

"What if I eat that fruit? It may give us a solution. I mean, something told me to look up, like a strange feeling, so maybe we need to go with it," he said.

"Well, you may have a plan there, Brac. It just might work. But the fruit may only work for the being that consumes it," she said. "But if it does, I hope you come back for me."

"If I don't remember anything else, it is that in the Arial World, anything is possible. I believe if I consume the fruit and think strongly about us getting out of here, it just may work. You did say the fruit was strong! So maybe if I climb and get it, that will be our way out," Brac said with confidence.

"Well," said Arbre. "We can give it a try."

Brac began to climb up the tree. "You think you can give me a little help?"

"I cannot control any part of this form. I'm afraid I might make a mistake that will cause you to fall. I don't want you to get hurt. We don't know what would happen if you were to die here," Arbre said with concern.

"Well, I guess I'm on my own with this one. I'll get the fruit, I promise you. We will get out of here." As Brac climbed the tree, he really began to notice how high it was. When he looked down, he was only about six feet up. "This is going to take forever," he muttered.

"Just be careful. I don't want you to get hurt for the sake of helping me. Even though you're in this world, you can get still hurt. Trust me—I know."

As Brac continued to climb, he noticed something else—Arbre was even wider than she had seemed when he was on the ground.

"Something wrong, Brac?" Arbre asked.

"It's nothing. I'm just trying to overcome the size. You're huge!"

"I'm the same size as the one I fell from, but the difference between you and me is I'm used to climbing these giants. It was the fruit that did me in." She giggled. "I probably would have survived the fall. My people are very, very strong."

Brac continued to climb and climb and climb. "I'm almost there," he told himself.

"Remember, Brac, do not eat the fruit while you're up there. That's how I died!"

Suddenly, something ran across Brac's hand as he grabbed the fruit. "What the…!?" said Brac. "What was that?"

"Are you okay up there?" Arbre asked.

But it was too late. A strange creature appeared. "I am he who seeks the fated one," hissed the snakelike creature. It regarded Brac cynically, drawing closer along the branch. "You have the clair qualities I seek."

"What are you?" Brac asked as his head began to sway from side to side. The fear drained from Brac's body as his gaze met those hypnotic eyes.

"What do you fear, boy?" the creature asked.

"I—I don't know."

"Not little ol' me, huh?" it said.

"I-I—" stuttered Brac.

"Well, you must be afraid of something; you're stiff as stale bread, young one," the creature said. "Let's play a game, shall we?"

It was quickly interrupted by a shout. "Brac, what is going on up there!?" yelled Arbre.

But Brac was still in a trance.

"Eat the fruit, boy. Eat the fruit," the creature demanded.

When Brac took a bite and nothing immediately happened, the serpent slithered away quickly.

"Brac! Brac!" yelled Arbre. "Are you okay up there!?"

Brac came back to his senses. "Huh, what the… Arbre!" he shouted.

"You weren't answering me. I called your name multiple times. What's going on up there?"

"I… I don't know," answered Brac.

"Well, do you have the fruit?"

"The fruit?"

"Yes, the fruit."

Brac looked around and found the fruit in the palm of his hand. "I do have the fruit, but it looks like somebody took a nice chunk out of it."

"A nice chunk! Brac, please tell me that you didn't eat that fruit while you were up there!"

But it was too late. Brac couldn't remember what had happened. He had been bamboozled. He began to feel very unusual. There were colors everywhere, waving like a loose rainbow. The limb he was sitting on even became wavy. The power of the fruit was changing everything.

"Brac!" Arbre's voice deepened and slowed.

Brac lost his balance. He fell off the limb like a dead man, limp and lifeless. Everything around him began to turn black.

Chapter 12

The Void

His eyes opened to pure darkness, not seeing even a speck of light. He was dazed and confused yet again.

"Brac!" came an unknown voice from the distance. "Get up off your keister. You're too strong for the weakness you're showing!" A figure came into the light.

"Mrs. de… Tunne," he whispered softly and slowly. While he was trying to gather himself, the name had come to him in pieces.

"There is no place for weakness here, my boy. You are in a hell of a doozy—I cannot lie about that. It is going to be hard, but you will pull through… I can feel it."

Then Brac began to get up. "Why do I keep ending up in weird places? And where is Arbre?"

"Well, you will have to train to get back to her, and to many others. The fruit that you ate brought you here. This is the place of creation, and you have been sent here for a reason," she said with a smile. "But that fruit that you ate was pure melaton. That's like devouring the power of a god! The fruit is full of power. Most are too weak to handle it, but you survived its great power! You have something hidden deep inside of you that protected you from the torture of the dark side of the universe. You're lucky you have your inner light—without it, you would be doomed!"

She gave him a hard stare. "You're lucky. The horrors of the universe are far more terrifying than anything that you have ever been through! We are here to help you become a warrior. Remember when I mentioned the clair?" she asked.

"Clair? Yes, I remember."

"Well, the clair is your perception, power, weakness, speed, spirit—everything that can become better is your clair. It's really just short for clarity, the ability to see clearly without anything blocking your vision. Your clair can help you form a tangible goal and then give you a path where you can go beyond." Then she asked, "Brac, what is your goal?"

Brac closed his eyes. Unbelievably, when he opened them, his life flooded around him in a clear sight. Things that he didn't know and did know traveled everywhere as fast as time itself. He understood it all. "My way, my way is to right all wrongs and to only live by the laws of the universe."

Femme de Tunne could do nothing but smile.

Chapter 13

Rotten Apple

As the last words of his declaration faded into the Void around them, an apple appeared, sitting in the space by his head as if perched on an invisible table. *Weird how this world works—is this even a world?*

"Hungry?" Brac asked Femme de Tunne.

"It's for you. You look hungry," she said.

"Well, thank you!"

"Eat up!"

"What, did I not have enough melaton already?" He smirked.

"Just eat the darn thing! It'll fill you up just enough."

Brac took a huge bite and disgust contorted his features. Rotten apple pieces burst from his mouth as he coughed. "What the—!" He spat to one side. "Why—ugh—would you give me a rotten apple?" Bursts of spit punctuated his words as he tried to get rid of the awful taste.

"To teach you a lesson about your thoughts. Before you go any further, you have to learn how to focus on having clean thoughts. Now, don't get me wrong—everything isn't as it seems. I curse, and I get angry, but it's how you balance it out that matters. Never let the negative overcome the positive. That apple was an example of a mind full of negativity. Corrupted, useless, bad, and rotten. Now, would you rather have that one, or this one?"

Another apple appeared in his hand.

"Give it a try."

Brac eyed the apple with caution, grabbed it, and slowly sank his teeth into it with a satisfying crunch. It was succulent, fresh, and not rotten!

"Now, isn't that better?" asked Tunne.

"Sure in the heck is!" Brac said with his mouth full.

"That's the positive mind! You can create many beautiful things with it, but be careful, for what you think will manifest into reality. You can start with this apple seed. I want you to make it grow into a ripe apple. You can have as much time as you like." She placed the seed in his hand, then began to vanish into the darkness. "I'll know when you're done. See you soon."

"Wait! W-what? Come back, aye! Tunne! Tunne! What kind of teacher are you!" He shouted, "You're supposed to be here helping me!" He fell to his knees in anger. "Stupid apple, stupid place, stupid! Stupid! *Stupid*!"

Suddenly, the seed began to sprout! It began to take the form of an apple, but even as it grew, it was starting to rot. It began to dry up and crack quickly.

"What in the world?" said Brac. "How did I—?" He was clueless. "All I said was stupid… Oh, negative brings about negative!" He then continued on. "Stupid apple, go away!"

What happened amazed him. The apple disintegrated before his eyes, leaving behind nothing but the original seed.

"Okay, maybe if I concentrate on what I want, I can make the seed transform… Okay… Give me a bright, juicy, purple apple!"

The seed shook, and shook, then grew into a giant black apple!

"Wow! It worked!" he said. "But it's black. I wonder if it's rotten." He sank his teeth into its flesh and found it tasted like no apple he'd ever eaten before. Sweet, juicy, and tangy—it was so wonderful that he closed his eyes and felt like he was floating in the clouds. When he opened his eyes, he found himself literally floating in a beautiful blue sky filled with clouds of every color.

"What, am I still in the Void?" he asked himself.

"You are always in the Void," said a familiar voice.

"Tunne! Where did you come from?" he asked.

"I never left," she said.

"But you vanished in the dark!"

"Oh, did I?" She eyed the multicolored sky. "Get your head out of the clouds. I want to show you something."

"What's that?" asked Brac. He heard heavy breathing and feet splashing through puddles of water, seeming to get closer with each step. He saw something that frightened him… *It's Artiest, but what is he doing here? And how did he get here?* Brac was trembling but shook it off enough to stand up. He braced himself. "Do I have to fight him now?"

"Don't judge a book by its cover," said Tunne.

As soon as she said those words, the strangest thing happened. Artiest shrank in size, his scars fading and death-defying gaze disappearing. He was a mere child. And he stopped right in front of Brac and just stared into his eyes.

"He cannot see you," said Tunne. "You're in a completely different dimension."

"Well, why is he staring at me?"

"He's not staring at you," she said. "He's staring behind you."

Brac slowly turned around to see a bunch of dead bodies lying behind him. "Oh crap!" He jumped up from a kneeling position. "What happened?"

"Watch and see, boy. You talk too much. Now I'm going to tell you a story. Watch as I explain." The Void then filled up, and she began the story of Artiest.

Chapter 14

Art and War: The Path of the Warrior! Artiest's Story!

With fire blazing all around him, the burning of flesh filled the air and his nostrils. Shouts of aches and pain from men, women, and children flooded into his ears. Everything and everyone he loved had been destroyed. "Why?" he asked as tears ran down his face.

"Little one!" came a smooth, deep voice. "The last to survive is the strongest."

He looked up and saw a man with black-and-gold armor on. He had a strong gray face, long black hair, and red eyes that reflected the flames like twin mirrors.

"Come with me!"

He was only twelve years old and had been turned heartless toward life in an instant, just as fast as the fire ate away at his everything. So he went, asking no questions, carrying a cold heart.

The man who had taken him away was a very strong man, but Artiest didn't know a thing about him. Mrs. Tunne explained as the memory of young Artiest trailed after the armored man. He was one of the most treacherous and powerful beings to ever exist: King Diyar Vincitor. Artiest's people were very isolated from others. His father taught him their family art, Harmony of the Graceful Spirit, which was a very powerful fighting style. It required a practitioner to be in tune with every aspect of their being: the mental, the physical, and the spiritual.

Vincitor was on his path of world domination to be well known and feared. He hated the sun; his first goal was to bring pain and suffering to the world so the negative energy could darken the sky and their hearts. He knew about those secrets and used them to his full capability.

He made Artiest suffer. For several days, he denied Artiest access to food, water, light, and companionship, breaking and murdering his mind.

Brac couldn't help it any longer. "But why?! Why did Vincitor want him?"

"Just listen," she said quietly.

Young Artiest never complained, never really begged to be set free. He just endured everything he was dealt. One day, Vincitor sent in one of his minions, just a weak one, to test Artiest. The minion was arrogant, immediately slapping and spitting on the boy, calling him weak, saying that his people deserved to be slaughtered, and revealing how he killed many of them with pleasure. He kicked Artiest in the groin. Artiest fell. The man said, "You're nothing but a piece of worthless meat," and laughed loudly.

In the moment of his belligerent laughter, the ground began to tremble. "What the hell!" shouted the minion. And with a sickening crack, the minion swallowed his own teeth.

Everyone had a beast within them, but it took another beast to bring it out.

The door swung open and slammed against the opposite wall, and Vincitor stepped through. A shiver went up Brac's spine.

"You killed my lackey," Vincitor said. With a smirk, he crouched to Artiest's level. "You're a very good prospect, you know. What did you do to make this man swallow his teeth?"

Brac took a deep breath.

"I tried to kill 'im…" Artiest said.

"What was that punch you used?"

"It was just a punch. No style, no grace…"

"I know someone trained you. What is your name?" Vincitor demanded.

"Who destroyed my village? Was it you?" Artiest asked as he stared into Vincitor's eyes.

"It was Brac; he's a rebel. He travels around like a street rat, lying and deceiving people, stealing their styles and wiping out everything and everyone. If you want revenge, you'll have to train before challenging him," said Vincitor.

"That monster!" Artiest shouted, pulling his chains so hard that his fastenings cracked.

"I tried to stop him, but the coward ran," Vincitor said with a wicked smile.

"He taught me all I know, but now I'll have to slaughter him like he did my people. They didn't deserve that!" He broke free from the chains and slammed his fists against the ground, cracking it.

"I'll train you; you can defeat him. Chop his head off, and take it as a trophy! Your hate will make you stronger. Your vengeance will guide you. I will mold you."

Artiest looked up at Vincitor with his good eye. "I'm going to kill him," he said. "Brac will die!"

"He fed into Vincitor's lie!" said Tunne.

Artiest trained and trained. Then he started going on missions for Vincitor, assassinating the best of the best. By the young age of fourteen, he had killed many lords and great warriors, both secretly and face-to-face. He was greatly feared by the age of seventeen. No one dared to challenge him in combat. But he could not find the man he sought.

Year after year passed by and still no Brac. But Artiest grew stronger and stronger. No one really gave him any trouble, and he conquered land mass after land mass. At the age of twenty-three, he was a master of the body.

One day, when he was traveling on a mission, he felt a very strong clair. "Who's there? I can feel you."

A man appeared. "Artiest. How are you?"

Artiest could not make out who the man was because he stood in the shadows. "Who are you?"

"So, you don't remember me?" he said. "Why, you don't know your own father?"

Artiest said, "My father's dead; he was killed a long time ago."

He said, "That man wasn't your father. He existed as a decoy. They were just trying to protect you from my legacy… I am your father!" And he made his way into the little light that shone.

"Brac!" Artiest said viciously. "You son of a—!" And he charged him.

"Why are you so angry, son?" Brac Sr. asked.

"You destroyed my home and murdered my people!"

Brac Sr.'s expression changed, concern overtaken by horror, and underneath that, a simmering rage. "What?! Who told you that?"

"Just know I've been training all my life to kill you!"

"Enough!" Brac Sr. demanded, and he punched Artiest so hard in the gut that he collapsed. "You need more training, son. And I have an idea who put those lies in your head."

Artiest coughed up blood. "I'm not your son, you piece of trash. And no one lied to me!" He tried to stand but could not.

"You won't be able to get up for a while after that blow. We will meet again. I have something else to tend to," Brac Sr. said angrily, and then sped off.

Artiest screamed, "Come back, you coward!" before fainting dead away.

When Artiest woke, he lay down for a long time in thought. Was the man he had trained all his life to kill telling the truth? Vincitor was a conqueror, and Brac was said to be a murderer, but was Vincitor the murderer? He was highly confused. The only thing he could do was find Brac once more…

Chapter 15

Father, Son, and Truth

"So what will happen to Artiest?" Brac asked.

"Well, what do you think will happen to you?"

"I… I really don't know? But when they were fighting, he looked right at me. Did he actually see me?" He was curious to know.

"He felt you. You have to remember that Artiest's life was, and still is, based upon godly structure. Because he was always training and always suffering, his senses were highly enhanced. Putting your mind and body through that type of suffering is going to break you and rebuild you. Some die during hardships, but the ones who make it through break barriers," she said.

"I want to become strong too, Tunne!"

"You will be because your real training starts now."

The Void changed again, transforming into a giant grassy area. It had a waterfall, fruit trees, and giant mountains—one of which was so big that the peak vanished into the sky. "This is your training ground. You will stay here for one full year under hard, extreme conditions," she said.

"Alone?" he asked.

"Well, you will have company, but it won't be me."

Brac was ecstatic. "Who will it be?"

"Look behind you," she said.

When he turned around, he thought his eyes were deceiving him. It was Brac's father! "F-Father…" he stuttered.

"I'll leave you two be. Later." Tunne smiled, and then slowly vanished.

"Ah, the son born on the day of my death. Nice to finally meet you," he said with a smirk.

"You mean the day you were murdered!" Brac replied.

"Hm, not exactly. It was more like a sacrifice. It was all staged by your brother and me," he said. "I let him kill me, for the sake of you and your mother, and for the fate of every world out there."

Brac was speechless. He was finally getting the truth.

"After Artiest attacked me in the forest, he came and found me and stayed with me until around the time when you were born. He went back to Vincitor and told him he had found me in a village that wasn't even worth destroying. But he was going to kill me. Artiest told Vincitor he overheard me saying that I would be there for a while, so he'd kill me soon. But keep in mind, he never said a word about seeing me before. Vincitor knew nothing about the bond we had created. I had gotten my son back! But in the end, I had to die by his hands. That's okay, though. It was worth the sacrifice. Plus, it will be safer for me to train you here. The first world is too dangerous."

"Now, what we need to do is test your strength first." He pointed at a rock about a quarter of a mile away. "Go pick up that rock, and bring it to me."

"I don't know. That rock looks awful heavy," said Brac.

"It's just a hundred pounds, son. Go on over and lift it. I know you can!"

His father's faith in him overpowered his doubts, sending new energy coursing through him. "Yeah, I can pick it up!" He made his way to it and began to lift it up with all his might. "I… got… it!" he grunted as he struggled.

"You got it, son!"

Brac had gotten his arms around the rock, but he could barely rise from a squatting position, even as his father encouraged him.

"Now walk over here with it!" Brac Sr. shouted. "It's not that far, son!"

With a growl of effort, Brac barely made it back to his father without dropping the rock. "That was… the hardest thing… I've ever done!" He collapsed.

"Not too bad, but watch this." Brac Sr. grabbed the hundred-pound rock with both hands, crouched, and tossed it a hundred feet into the air!

"What in all death—?" shouted Brac. "What the hell are you made of!?" He couldn't believe his eyes as the rock flew higher.

"The same thing as you." Brac Sr. laughed. He flexed an arm and cast a speculative glance up at the rock. "You know," he said reflectively. "Yeah, I think that actually weighed two hundred pounds."

That made Brac think. "I just picked up two hundred pounds! What's next?"

"Well, next is you climbing that tree to get us some food and watching out for that rock," his father said.

With a sound like the boom of thunder, the rock crashed into the earth.

As Brac recovered from the aftershock of the rock's impact, he tried to focus on the tree his father had indicated. To his horror, he found it to be at least sixty feet tall. With the results of his last attempt to climb a tree still fresh in his mind, he took a healthy step back. "But can't you jump super high, like you did in that fight with Artiest, and get up there yourself?"

Brac Sr. said, "Everything that I'm used to doing, you will do. Unless you want to go back home knowing that you could have been strong enough to defeat Vincitor and save your world, but you decided to go back as a weakling instead. Your choice."

Chapter 16

Courage and Persistence

"Now, I'll nap while you fetch that food, son. You'll be all right. Courage and persistence are the keys to life." He said that and fell straight asleep.

Brac looked at him and then the tree. "Why does everyone keep doing this to me?" He glanced over to his sleeping father, then let his eyes travel up the tree again. "Oh well. I have to get stronger." So he grabbed the first piece of bark and began climbing. Step by step, he took his time, not looking down or thinking negative thoughts. But as he got higher, the flashbacks began to kick in. He started to wonder about Arbre. *Where could she be? Is she safe?* "Arbre, one of my first friends in this wild journey." He hadn't noticed he was halfway up the tree already, but he looked down and had no fear of falling. "I'm going to get stronger, and I will find you."

"No need!" came a soft voice. "I'm right here, Brac."

Brac did not know where to look.

"Look up, silly."

When he did so, he found a girl sitting on a branch a little ways above him. "Arbre! How did you—?"

"Magic!" she said. "Come on up and eat with me!"

He hurried on up and took a seat beside her.

"You climbed up here with no problem, huh?" Then she giggled. "Fruit?" She handed him a purple apple, and he bit into it.

"Mmm, strange. It tastes like the apple I ate earlier! Amazing!" he said. "So you got here by magic?"

"Yes, I found my magic charm bracelet. It can take me to safety in desperate times, and I thought about you. I can't go home; it won't let me. I have no idea why not, but I'll figure a way to get back sooner or later," she said confidently. "So, what are you doing here?"

"Well, I'm here training with my dad."

"You mean that man down there? Then why is he asleep?"

Brac looked down at him. "I guess he's just tired."

"Or he's trying to see if you can handle yourself. My father used to do the same thing. He would send me into the forest for wood alone and see if I could get—ah, catch—get it, and might I remind you we have many beasts that lurk in our woods. They were tasty!"

Brac wondered, *Is she stronger than me?* He knew darn well he couldn't tussle a beast. He wanted to ask her so badly to climb down and see if she could pick up that rock! "Hey," he said. "Let's go down. I have to wake my dad up and tell him I have the food."

They began to descend to the bottom of the tree. She was so fast! The sight woke his competitive spirit, and he went down the tree like a squirrel.

"Wow! You're fast!" she said.

"I don't even know how I did that." He looked at his dad, who was still asleep. "I guess I'll show him later. But anyway, I think it was the fruit that made me so fast."

"Son, that was you!"

They both jumped. Brac Sr. had spooked them a little.

"That's some weird-looking fruit." He bit into it. "Mmm, very, very good! Who made this?" he asked.

"I think I did, but the one I made was a lot bigger. I don't know, but anyway, I want you to meet my friend. Her name's—"

"Arbre!" Brac Sr. cut in. "I know her name. Hey, Arbre, give this rock a try. Pick it up and walk from here to that tree."

Brac thought his father was reading his mind.

"Okay!" She grabbed the rock with both hands and headed toward the tree. She was speed walking, visibly not struggling with the weight at all.

Amazed, he thought, How is she this strong?

"Courage and persistence, son. Courage and persistence," said Brac Sr. "She was not born like that, but she was trained very well. But without her father, she was lost. You can be just as strong in a matter of time."

When she got back, she tossed the rock backward over her head, and it flew at least twelve feet.

"Well, son, looks like you have a training partner!" he said.

"Man, I haven't done some work like that in a while!" She looked at Brac and smiled. "Wanna see something amazing?"

"Umm, sure," he said.

"I haven't done this in a while either." She closed her eyes and grew still. What happened next was stunning! Before Brac's disbelieving eyes, her feet lifted from the ground.

"She can fly too!" he said. "That's amazing. How is that even possible?" He watched as she flew all around them at a very high speed.

"Brac!" she said as she went in circles. "I know you can do it too. It's so easy!"

Brac thought, *This girl! What is she thinking that she can float above ground...* He had entered a place where every and anything was possible!

"While the two of you were on your uncle's planet, her true potential was inhibited by her fear, but she's unafraid now, and she wants to change things. One day, you'll be the same. She was kept from her true potential because of her sadness, which threw off her magic. But she found out that she has a chance to go back home. And so do you!"

Brac watched her as she flew with excitement. "I want to tell her everything, but I don't want to spoil her happiness. I'll just wait."

"Brac, grab hold." She reached out her hand.

"Um... Okay, but don't go too high or too fast!"

She looked at him, smiled, and said, "I won't!" She crossed her fingers behind her back, but Brac couldn't see that until it was too late.

They took off slowly, floating only a couple of feet in the air. "Not too bad!" he said.

"Nope! Not at all," she said. "But I have something to show you."

Brac looked at her. "What's that?"

"How it really feels to fly!" She took him straight up in the air, fast enough that tears streamed from his eyes.

Brac yelled, "What are you doing?! This is not what I asked for!" They were so high up he could not see his father anymore, nor the trees, but he did see the mountaintop. He thought he saw something glowing out the corner of his eye, but as all his attention was focused on not dying, he couldn't check. Then back down they went, hurtling toward the ground at full speed. "No, no, no, no, no!" he chanted.

She paid him no mind and continued to plummet!

"You're going to kill us!" he shouted.

With an earthshaking boom, they hit the ground hard—dirt flew everywhere, covering the scene. When the dust cleared, Brac found himself cradled in Arbre's arms like a baby. His father stood a few feet away, visibly unbothered despite being covered in a layer of detritus.

"See, that wasn't so bad," she said.

"You people are crazy!" he screamed. "All of you!" Then he paused and said, "I absolutely love it!" His heart was hammering in his chest, and he could barely breathe, but he had never felt so alive before.

"Well, looks like it's time to get serious!" said Brac Sr.

Chapter 17

Getting Rid of a Burden

"Son!" Brac Sr. shouted. "Wake up and stretch!"

Brac jumped up in an instant. "What? Huh? Who?" he said with a jolt. "What's wrong?"

"Training starts now!"

When Brac looked around, he saw it was nighttime, and the stars were plentiful. "What in the hell," he muttered.

"Look, Arbre is already up and stretching," said Brac Sr.

"Brac, you should make this a part of your daily routine!" she hollered.

"Now get up, son. You need to move that rock."

"Move a rock? But why is that so important?" Brac asked.

"You must think moving that rock is just a waste of time. Honestly, son, that wasn't even the warm-up. Every day, until you can do this exercise with ease, you will wake up and carry that rock from here to the falls."

Brac looked upstream to where his father pointed. "What falls?"

"You'll see when you get there. Just follow the river. And you must bring it back every day. If you can't make it back, you stay wherever you are. Arbre will accompany you."

Brac looked at Arbre and said, "Stretch first, huh? I guess so."

"I can show you how to stretch properly, if you're up for it," she said with a smile.

Brac agreed.

"You see, you have to stretch before doing any type of tough physical activity. You don't want to pull a muscle," she said. "You have to concentrate on your breathing as well. Breathe deeply and steadily as you move."

Brac actually felt great after following along with Arbre, but after the warm-up stretching, the boulder and the promise of growing stronger still waited for him. "Well," he said, "here goes." He strained his muscles as he struggled to pick the mini boulder up off the ground. Beside him, Arbre picked hers up like it was only an ounce. "Dad, if she is so much stronger, why is she lifting the same weight as I am?"

"Well," said Arbre, "Brac does have a point! I would like to get stronger too, sir!"

Brac Sr. looked around and nodded toward a bigger boulder. "There, that's your boulder then, Arbre." He led her to the same rock he'd hurled into the air.

"Okay!" she said with spunk as she hopped on over.

"Hopefully, she can get her arms around it," Brac said with dismay as she squared up with the rock.

"Hmm, it's kind of big, but here goes!"

To Brac's surprise, Arbre lifted the rock with little strain. "Okay, Brac, ready?" It was so big she had to peep her head to the side just to see.

"I guess."

And they took off, Brac stumbling after Arbre's easy stride.

Chapter 18

Words of Encouragement

Along the way, after Brac's father had vanished in the distance, Brac began to struggle.

"You okay?" Arbre asked.

"No. It's getting heavier and heavier," he said.

"Just a little bit longer, and we'll take a break," she said with a smile.

"I know I'm holding you back," said Brac.

"No, you're not. Don't think like that. I'm here to help you. You will get stronger. Just think about something else, or better yet, talk about something else. It will help take your mind off the pain," she said.

"Well, I did want to," he grunted, "talk about something." He strained to get his words out.

"Drop it," she said.

With a thud, his boulder sank into the ground.

She carefully put hers down and sat on it.

Brac plopped down on the ground. "Is it possible for me to save a whole world?" he asked. "I mean, it seems as though everyone I've met is so certain I can, but I don't even know where to start." He looked up at her. "What would you do, Arbre?"

"Well, first off, I would do what you're doing now: keep training. You must have an understanding of the problem that needs to be solved. Then from there, you can figure out the best way to solve it."

Brac took a moment to think. "The problem? The problem is… freedom," he muttered. "But how do I do that? How do I bring freedom to others?"

Arbre looked at him, smiled, and said, "You have to lead by example. If you're the savior, it all starts with you."

Brac smiled. "So I have to free myself."

"Yes! You have to rid yourself of the idea that the world is set in stone. When I was a tree, I could see how people shaped the world with just their will. The universe answers to us, not to some higher power. We're not bound to our fates, but we have to have faith in ourselves. That's what makes everything possible." She leaned forward like she was bestowing a great secret upon him. "All you have to do is believe, Brac!"

Those words were so powerful that they made Brac regain strength and hope. He picked up the boulder and carried it with renewed determination. "Let's go, Arbre!" he declared.

Arbre leaped to her feet. "That's the spirit!" she cheered, lifting her own boulder again.

They made their way to the falls.

Chapter 19

Welcome to the Jungle

"So we have to go through all of this?!" Brac was shocked at what lay before them. It was a dark, dense jungle. "I've seen enough of this in the first world! I can't do it! I can't!" Brac took a step back. Any positive feelings he'd had at the start of the exercise were curling up and dying. There was no way he'd set foot in something so dark and dangerous.

The flashbacks came back. He saw himself in the forest of Hofu running toward his mother's voice: "Go back, Brac! It's a trap!"

Arbre looked at him. "Stop, Brac! That is what you can't do!" she screamed. "Don't let them take your mind. Freedom, freedom is what you want! We're moving forward, Brac! Tell those demons to go to hell!"

He looked at her before blinking hard, his eyes suddenly hot and itchy. "But is freedom what I will get?"

"Brac, your eyes! They're red!" She reached toward him, but before her fingers could even graze his shoulder, she snatched her hand back as if burned. "Listen, whatever happens, you're going to make a change! Don't give in, Brac! Fight it, please! There's something terrible inside you. It's strong, and it's fierce, but you're going to have to be stronger! I know you can do it!"

"I—I feel like I'm about to go crazy!" he shouted. "Screw this!" He then picked up the two-hundred-pound boulder and threw it through the jungle. It flew so far that they lost sight of it.

Breathing heavily, he slowly began to calm down. "What the hell was that!?" He was utterly confused. "It was like I was fighting against myself."

"Brac, you have something inside of you that you need to learn how to control," she said. "True freedom is the key to life, and if you become enslaved to wrong, you will never become a master of right! There are many things you need to learn."

They stared at each other as Brac tried to understand her words.

As they made their way to the edge of the jungle, Brac remembered when he had gotten lost in the dark forest of Hofu.

It had happened when he was younger, about eight years of age. Everyone had gone crazy looking for him. His mother, her friends, their children—everyone searched for Brac. One of his friends had told him not to go into the forest, but he hadn't listened. The boy had gone back and told Brac's mother, and she went crazy. They'd lit torches and rushed to the forest's edge. No one ever went into the forest alone because of the legend that gave it its name—Hofu meaning simply "fear"—but when Brac vanished, they'd had no choice.

Meanwhile, Brac had gone deeper and deeper into the forest. As a little boy, he'd felt like something was calling, guiding, and watching him.

He had crept slowly through the eerie jungle, not worried about the creatures that could gobble him up in one mouthful or poison him with a single bite. Suddenly, he heard a loud purr and jumped. Not making out what it was, he had only seen a glimpse of the huge figure running through the trees. He'd seen something zoom behind it—something bright.

"Brac!" a voice had yelled from behind him. "Brac!"

The familiar cry had startled him from his reverie, and he looked back toward it. The pull to the figure in the trees faded, and he had given it one last glance before turning to the voice.

She had gathered all of the warriors to find him. "Brac!" She'd grabbed and hugged him. "What is wrong with you?" she'd shouted. "Don't you ever scare me like that again!"

He had looked at her and innocently said, "But, Mama, something's in there."

"Nothing is in there but danger. Haven't I told you that? Only warriors are allowed to go in and hunt, not children!" she'd said.

"But, Mama, whatever it wa—"

"Shut up," she had told him. "Don't you ever set foot in here again." She stood up and walked away.

He knew then to never go back.

"I—I just saw my past…" He held his head down.

"Why do you have your head down?" Arbre said. "We're in the jungle, you know. Keep your head up, Brac. There's plenty to see."

When he looked up, there must have been a million fireflies surrounding them.

"Look, this is what you will miss with closed eyes," she said.

These weren't like any other fireflies he'd seen before—in the first world, fireflies were rare and glowed yellow, but there, they glowed countless different colors.

"Wow!" he said.

"This is just the beginning; there's a whole new world out there! Your world. No one can change that for the better but you, Brac. Hold your hand out," she directed.

Brac slowly reached out to the swarm.

"Now, make them come to you."

"But how?" he asked. "I tried to make an animal come to me before, and it didn't work. Shakoora—the girl who asked me to do it—she said they sensed my fear. It was so strong that it scared all of them away."

"What do you have to fear, Brac?" she asked.

"I keep having these flashbacks from the first world, and they scare the crap out of me!"

She looked at him and said, "You're afraid of the word water, but you are an ocean."

That confused Brac. "What does that mean?"

"It means that you're afraid of the representation of something, even though it's just a representation of you. When you think of a word, you picture it, but it is not really tangible—you are!" she said. "Take the word 'fear,' for instance. You are frightened by a word, but in all truth, you are the origin, the beholder of that word. Before it was a word, it was a feeling, Brac! Get it?"

He looked at her and said, "So, you're saying that I'm fear itself?"

"Yes, we are all masters of our feelings and emotions. So, in times of chaos, you have to learn to control your feelings and your emotions, or you may find yourself in a heck of a doozy. Now, I want you to try again!" she said with a smile.

Brac took a few deep breaths and put his finger back out.

"Take your time. Show it you care."

What happened next humbled him. One firefly flew toward him, landed on his finger, and glowed brighter.

"You're doing it, Brac," she whispered. "You're doing it!"

Then another landed on his head, then another, and another.

"They trust you, Brac! So you need to trust in yourself. Letting your fears take over will continue to damage you. We're here to start over, not dwell on the past," she said with a smile.

They began to cover his whole body, every inch of it except his face.

"It's so beautiful," said Arbre. "Brac! You're floating!"

They began to slowly lift him, but not too high. "This feels so peaceful," he said with closed eyes. The wind from their wings cooled him down, and the warmth from their glow dried his sweaty clothes. "If this is how freedom feels," he said as he carefully spread his arms, "then count me in!" For the first time, he had no doubt, no worry, and no fear could conquer him. He was experiencing bliss for the first time, but a sudden pulse of energy ruined it.

In an instant, the fireflies dashed away, and Brac hit the ground. "Ouch! What's got them spooked?" he muttered.

"I come for the one named Brac!" said a deep voice.

"Show yourself!" Arbre shouted.

"Shut up, witch! I have no dealings with your kind! Boy, I want your body!"

Brac was shocked and a little confused. "You want my body? I don't swing that way, sir!"

When it came again, the voice was low with displeasure. "You idiot. Do you know who I am?"

"Look, I can't even see you, so how the hell am I supposed to know who you are?"

As if in response to his question, a boulder came flying out of the trees, aimed right for his head.

"Brac, move!" Arbre dove and blocked the rock with her shoulder. It spun away into the dirt.

"No, Arbre!" Brac sprang to his feet. In the direction of the voice, he shouted, "What's wrong with—"

"You!" the voice cut in. As he drew nearer and his features caught the light, Brac's breath caught in his throat. The man before him was his spitting image.

Chapter 20

Fearless: Fighting Demons!

"What!" Brac said with shock. "How is this even possible?"

The man before him could have been his twin—even after a second look, the similarity between them didn't fade. He was looking at a spitting image of himself.

"You idiot! You dare get rid of me?" His voice was raspy, and he was scowling. Unlike Brac, he was fierce looking, staring at him as if he wanted to kill him on the spot. If Brac hadn't already been dead, he was sure the look his mirror image was giving him would have put him six feet under.

"Brac!" Arbre called. "Watch him. He is very strong and ruthless! You don't want to fight him right now—he'll use manipulation to make you weak. He is a master of fear."

Brac looked back at her and said, "How do you even know all of this?"

Arbre shook her head. "I don't know. His eyes—they're just full of answers."

Brac gave her a look of disbelief. "What does that even mean?"

The other Brac's eyes glowed blood red, and Brac shivered at the sight. He only knew one other person with eyes like that: Vincitor. "Enough talk!" snapped the other Brac. "I've been trapped inside you for too long. I want that body, and I want it now!" He roared as he charged Brac with terrifying speed.

"Brac, no!" Arbre shouted. "Stay back!"

He replied, "This is my fight, and he won't be taking anything!" It seemed as though Brac had finally found his courage—he did not back down and instead raced toward his mirror image.

They clashed, going blow for blow, neither backing down. Their fists smashed into each other's flesh. Brac was taking more crushing blows than his evil counterpart.

"Brac," Arbre muttered. "He's going head-to-head with himself. That's crazy. He's actually holding his own, and my, he can take a punch—with rigorous training, who knows what would happen."

Suddenly, Brac fell to one knee, blood gushing from his nose and mouth.

"Are you okay?" Arbre tried to run to check on him, but he put his hand up to halt her.

He paused and took a deep breath before putting his fists back up. He wasn't backing down.

His counterpart grinned mischievously as he brushed his hand over his face, but that grin turned to surprise as he saw the blood streak on his hand. Brac's fingernails had carved a gash over his eye. "Hmm, not too many have made me bleed. You must be special," he said. "If you're so strong, I must have your body for my own! I still smell a piece of fear inside of you, and I will make it grow. I am a soul taker, created from your fears. This is my territory, and soon enough, you will be too! You won't be leaving with that body of yours!"

But it was as though Brac didn't hear him. He just stood there.

The soul stealer charged at him. "Get ready, you fool!" he shouted.

But Brac didn't budge one bit, even as the soul taker rushed in.

"Brac, move!"

But he didn't.

The soul taker's punch flew at Brac's face with terrible speed. Brac knew if that punch connected, it would probably cave in his skull. He was going to break Brac's face. "Now!" he said as his head went to the side, slipping the blow.

It hit… but Brac didn't fall; his mirror image did. "I-it worked." Brac collapsed.

"Are you okay?" asked Arbre.

"Yes, but I'm drained," he answered while taking a deep breath. "He just took a lot out of me. That was the hardest"—he paused to take another breath—"I've ever had to fight."

Suddenly, the body of the soul taker began to glow.

"Brac!" She held his head up. "Look, he's glowing!"

The body glowed bright yellow, a color like the sun, before curling up into a ball. With a flash of light sending dazzling rays out over the ground, it vanished.

"Brac, did you see that?" she asked.

But he was well asleep. She stared at him and smiled. "You did good. You proved you are a warrior, and you are fearless in tough times. Sleep well," she said. "We'll continue when you wake."

***

When Brac woke, he was confused as ever. "What? Arbre! Arbre!" he yelled.

"Huh? Oh Brac, you're awake." She had placed him in a tree and slept on the ground so if anything came, she could protect him.

"How did I get up here?" he asked.

"I put you there. You don't remember your fight?" she said. "I don't remember anything else." She scratched her head.

"So, what happened to the other me?"

She was shocked he really couldn't remember anything. "Well, you beat him! You were fighting fearlessly, and he got out of control and rushed into you. You timed him and slipped past. His attack barely grazed you, which explains the brush on your ear. You countered the counter you!" she said excitedly. "It was one of the best comebacks I have ever seen!"

Brac was astounded by what he heard. "I did?"

She said, "Well, let's make our way to the falls and then go back. We both need to wash off, and you're covered in blood."

He nodded his head, picked up his boulder, and continued the journey.

Chapter 21

Washing Away the Past

When they got to the falls, it was breathtaking. Everything was so beautiful. Brac hurried and dropped his boulder. He took a deep breath. "We did it," he said with pride.

"No, Brac, this is your journey. You did it!" She dropped her boulder. "Beautiful, isn't it?"

"Beautiful isn't the word," said Brac.

They stared at the way the water flowed into the plunge pool beneath. They could see straight to the bottom, where it was filled with shimmering fish, emeralds, and gold.

"The Arial World is very rich," he said.

"That's because riches don't matter here," she said.

"Well in my world, it's all that matters," he said.

"You can change that, you know. Just trust your journey and your heart. You're a good person, and you're very brave."

Brac smiled and said truthfully, "Thanks, no one has ever given me as many compliments as the people here. You guys have made me feel like somebody."

"Brac, you've always been somebody. Everyone has greatness within them. Sometimes a person needs a catalyst to help them."

He didn't know what that meant. "A catalyst?"

"It's like a spark to a fire, you know, getting it started!" she explained. "Without that spark, there is no flame. So, that's what a catalyst is. The beginning or start. You just needed a spark to start your fire; you're going to be blazing soon."

He smiled in return.

"Come on," she said. "Let's go to the top."

When they made it to the top of the falls, she said to him, "Now, everything that has happened is gone but not forgotten. So it's time to cleanse yourself of all of the mishaps and agony you have experienced. The best part about the pain is making it through. So you're going to take a dive into a new life. Let go of whatever is holding you back. When you jump off these falls"—she looked at him, her gaze deadly serious—"you will be freed from bondage!"

He turned to face the edge and walked toward it. The falls had to be at least eighty feet high, but he did not hesitate. He leaped off the cliff instantly, with Arbre coming right behind him. His life flashed before his eyes as he fell; everything from his birth to that very moment seemed to play out in midair, then he plunged into darkness.

Bursting out of the water, he took his first fresh breath of air.

As he reached toward the sky, Brac felt his body rise from the water, leaving him floating as comfortably in midair as he would in the pool below.

Arbre's laugh rang out by his ear. "Boy, you are something else."

As he wrapped his hand around a gem, a strong aura pulsed out from its core. As he surfaced, he came to a realization: "There's power in darkness!" he said while examining the jewel.

"Are you hungry?" Brac asked.

"Sure am," she said.

"Well, how about we head back to grab something?" he suggested.

"That sounds great!"

They climbed out of the falls, grabbed their boulders, and went off.

"You know, your dad will be very proud of you," she said. "You have proven you are a great warrior. I mean, you carried the rock, defeated a monster, and became free from your burden of fear! Fear still exists, but you have control over it, Brac."

"Yeah, I did do all of that, but it still isn't enough," he said without making any eye contact. "I have a long way to go; I'm not even close to his level. I know my father's strong, but I want to be stronger."

"Brac, notice how easily you're carrying that rock," she said. "You've gotten stronger than you think."

He hadn't even noticed he was carrying the boulder with ease, not straining one bit. "You're right, but my father can—"

"Enough about what he can do!" she cut in. "He trained to get there, and you have to also. Nothing comes easy. If it did, you wouldn't be here training to save your world. It would have never needed a savior if everything was easy," she said. "But it does, Brac."

He turned and looked into her eyes.

"You have to work hard to get strong. It won't be handed to you on a silver platter. Ask your father; he was not always the man is now. It took courage and persistence for him to evolve, and that took years of discipline and dedication. And what did he do after all of that?"

Brac narrowed his gaze.

"He did everything he could to protect his loved ones, and he trusts in you to do the same."

She was right: it was up to Brac. They had chosen him to carry the load.

"They all believe in you. *I* believe in you!" she said, her eyes welling with serenity. Arbre paused, seeming to look for something around them. "Before we get back, I have something to tell you." Her voice shook. "Something big is going on."

"What do you mean, something big?"

"The energy of the universe has not been right—there's a lot of bad energy out there. What happened to you the other day—that was weird! And then he just vanished after you defeated him. I don't know if he was a part of you at all or if he was just something wearing your face, but something isn't right. I'm sure of it."

When they returned to the meadow where they left Brac Sr., he came to greet them. "You made it back in one piece, huh?"

"Yeah, we ran into some small problems, but it wasn't anything that Brac couldn't handle," Arbre said.

"So, Brac handled it, huh?"

Brac ducked his head, blushing furiously. "Yes, sir, I handled it, and I did it well!" With renewed confidence, Brac raised his head.

"Well, you should be proud of yourself." He examined Brac again. "Hmm, I see you're carrying that boulder more easily. You two must have been through some stuff—nobody gets that strong that fast." Things got quiet for a moment. "Look," said Brac's father. "Something's going on. Arbre, am I right in guessing you feel the change?"

She looked at Brac, then his father. “Well, I did notice some changes in the energy of the universe, but what actually, I don’t know.”

“Well, Brac, that just makes the training you’re about to do even more intense. We don’t know what it is that’s coming, but I know one thing: it’s going to be big,” he said. “Even Bilge came by while you two were gone. He told me Vincitor has a lot to do with this. If you ask me, I think he is trying to bring forth a power that should not be tampered with, that fool.”

“Well, I want to continue to train with Brac! He’ll need all the help he can get,” said Arbre.

“Well, that sounds great, but you two are up for some great challenges ahead. We all are.”

Chapter 22

The Power of Training

Every day, Brac got stronger and stronger; training began to get easy for him. That two-hundred-pound rock became a three-hundred-pound rock, then a four-hundred-pound rock. He even caught up to Arbre in strength and knowledge. They trained together, ate together, talked together, studied together, and went on missions together. The two of them became inseparable friends as well as frightening opponents. Together, they were getting to a point where they would give Brac Sr. a run for his money. He and his father had gotten close—all three of them had, as a matter of fact. But no matter how much Brac learned, there was always going to be so much more for him to absorb.

A little over a year into his training, Brac's father called to him. "I need you to go on a mission."

"Okay, where are we going?" Brac asked.

"I'll need you to go alone."

Brac had never been on a mission alone before. "What's the mission?"

"Climbing that mountain," he said.

"Wait, so after all this time we've been here and that mountain's been there, now you want me to climb it? What's up there, anyway? What will climbing a mountain do for my training?" Brac didn't want to have to stop his training to climb a mountain. He couldn't help but think it sounded pointless. He was used to his routine.

"You'll see. I want to see you at the base first thing in the morning. Both of you can have a day off today." He got closer to Brac's face and said, "You thought going into the jungle was something. Wait until you do this."

Early in the morning, the suns rose, their rays catching in the morning dew and making the grass seem to glow. Their light woke the animals and the people alike, but Brac was already awake, standing at the base of the mountain and waiting for his father. "Where is he?" he said. "I've been here since dawn." He had no idea where his father was. He began to think it was some kind of joke. Maybe his father was making him wake up even earlier to see if he was really dedicated to his training. "Man, this is a load of crap!" He kicked the mountain.

"Oh really?"

Brac jumped—it was his father. "You finally made it, huh?" he said. "I've been here forever waiting on you! Where's Arbre?"

"I have her doing something else," he said. "You just focus on your training. You're about to go through more than you expect, son. Everything else was just a walk in the park compared to this."

Brac thought the old man was going crazy—there was no possible way climbing up a mountain would be comparable to working himself into the ground almost every day for over a year. "Okay, you actually have gone mad! No way can climbing a rock compete with the training that we've been doing!"

His father looked at him and said, "This rock is going to kick your butt." He laughed out loud. "Surely, you don't know what you're getting yourself into! You think I'll give you something easy? *You* must be mad! The fate of the universe is at stake, and you think I'm going to go soft on you?" Brac Sr. leaned closer and made a show of sniffing Brac's breath. "Have you been at the liquid melas with your uncle, son? Your brain seems to be malfunctioning."

Brac still couldn't really believe that climbing a rock would help him, but he kept his mouth closed because he had faith in his father and his tactics. "Okay, I'm ready," said Brac with annoyance.

"Okay, go—wait, wait, wait! I forgot to give you these."

Brac looked down and saw four gold rings his father was holding. "So you're giving me a gift before I leave. Aww, how sweet of you," he said.

"Here, these are for your wrists and ankles." Brac's father smiled. "Go ahead, try them on." He first put them on Brac's ankles, and then on his wrists. "Now you're all ready to go."

Brac turned around and jumped to get a boost up the mountain. Midair, a weight seized his limbs and dragged him to the ground. "What the heck! These things feel like they weigh a ton," he said.

"They only reflect the energy you put out. If you punch with five hundred pounds of force, these will weigh your body down with the corresponding weight. So, with that being said, you'll be doing extreme resistance training."

Brac understood why he said the challenge would be difficult. "So if I throw a punch, ha!" He threw it hard. The weight of his bracelets doubled immediately, sending him to the ground with a muffled thud.

"You'll have to learn how to control it. It may take you a few days to climb to the top," Brac Sr. said. "If you make it at all, that is. And if you don't, use this." He gave him a black stone. "If you get too exhausted and want to give up, just eat these." His father had three round ruby-red things that looked like stones. "These are sweet stones. They look hard, but once you place them in your mouth, they break down easily. They're full of protein and will give you an amazing boost."

"Hmph, I won't be needing these," he said with confidence.

"Just keep them. I want to see if those words you speak are true. Trust me, the higher you get, the more you'll want to come back down."

Brac had never felt more confident, bracelets or not. He knew there was no way he would back down. "Okay, here I go, no turning back!"

And he began to climb. He went slowly so the bracelets would not be much of a burden. "I got this!" he said. Trying to learn how to control his power wasn't easy with those bracelets on. Halfway up the base, he had to stop. "This isn't going to be as easy as it seemed. I thought it was going to be useless. But this might be the ultimate test." He knew he was in for a doozy. When he looked back, his father was gone. He was on his own.

Chapter 23

The G.O.A.T.

He tried to shake off his fear. "You know what? I'm no weakling. I'm acting like I've never done anything I thought I couldn't do," he said, trying to console himself even as his fingers trembled with nerves. "This is just another way to prove I'm great—that I'm already at the top of this mountain!"

He clapped the bracelets together, and they reflected, but this time, he did not budge. "I'm Brac Guider, and I will be a legend!" he shouted and began again to climb. The bracelets were doing their duty, but so was he. He was gripping and clawing so hard that he was engraving prints in the stone. "I don't know what's at the top, but I'm going for it!" He was indifferent to the weight of gravity upon him.

He had climbed so high that when he looked down, all he saw were clouds that circled the mountain. Then, something smashed against his ribs with a hideous crack, sending him flying sideways and crashing onto a ledge. He began clawing to find purchase in the rock before he fell, and that wouldn't be pretty.

"What was that?" When he looked up, wheezing from the hit, he saw perched on another ledge a massive, muscular goat. It was covered with black hair, and incredible black horns curled around its face. Its golden eyes glared into his soul, and Brac knew he was in for a fight.

"Why are you on my mountain?" the goat asked with a very deep voice, sounding like thunder.

"I-I mean no harm. I'm on my final training mission. I was sent by my father, Brac Guider."

The goat looked at him and frowned, blowing steam from his nostrils. Hanging from his flaring nostrils was a gold ring, and gold bracelets similar to Brac's were looped around his legs. "Hmm, so Brac Guider sent you, huh?" he asked.

"Yes, he did, but he didn't tell me this was your mountain," said Brac.

"Hmph, that big imbecile! He created me and didn't tell you about me!" he said with anger.

"No, sir, Mr. Goat, I mean, sir!" He stumbled over his words.

"I am the Goat of Alta Terra, the master of this mountain! I am the G.O.A.T., and no one gets past without my consent!"

Brac knew the G.O.A.T. was serious, so he got into his fighting stance. "All right, look, I don't know what it takes to get your consent, but I'm ready for whatever!" he said.

The G.O.A.T looked at him and began to beat the mountain with his hoof, creating a small landslide. "You dare show such disrespect toward me, and on my mountain!" he said angrily. "I'm going to knock you off into oblivion!" The G.O.A.T. charged him, but Brac was smart enough to drop off the ledge and catch himself.

"Stop running from me, you coward!" screamed the G.O.A.T.

Brac was hanging off the ledge. The G.O.A.T. came back at full speed—Brac had to think quickly. He swung off the ledge and grabbed the G.O.A.T. by the horns.

"How dare you!" he screamed. "I'm going to smash you to pieces!"

The G.O.A.T. was in a rage. All Brac could do was hold on, but as he did, he started to talk. "You know, you ought to calm down," he said calmly. "You're going crazy over a kid climbing a rock."

That infuriated the G.O.A.T., and he started smashing against the mountain even harder. "I'm going to destroy you, boy!" He kicked at the rocks so hard that sparks flew from under his hooves.

That was it for the G.O.A.T.; he started gouging a hole into the mountain. When it got too deep, the G.O.AT. began to furiously slam himself against the stone, crushing Brac's legs between the furry, muscled frame and the unforgiving stone. The thudding of their bodies against the mountain sent shudders of pain throughout Brac's body, and he leaped from the G.O.A.T.'s back to escape the blows.

"Come on!" Brac yelled.

He punched the G.O.A.T. right in the nose. The bracelets kicked in, piling more weight on top of his limbs, but Brac didn't let up. He kept on swinging. The G.O.A.T. seemed to be getting desperate, hitting Brac with his hooves and headbutting him. They were making the hole even bigger, constantly bashing each other!

Brac grabbed the G.O.A.T.'s horns again, and they struggled to overpower one another. "You know what!" Brac shouted. He began banging his head against the G.O.AT.'s. Driving toward dizziness, he picked his arms up one by one and started continuously smashing the bracelets as hard as he could against the G.O.A.T.'s head, which sounded like gunshots. "You big stupid furball!" When the G.O.A.T.'s struggling slowed, Brac leaned over him and let the full energy of both bracelets come crashing down onto his skull. His body lay there, stiff, in a giant crater. Brac knelt over him, with a knee pressed against his throat. What a fight it had been!

Brac eased off the G.O.A.T.'s neck and stood up. "Now I'm the G.O.A.T.!" he said proudly.

"You have defeated me," he said. "I give you my consent." He struggled to get up.

"Let me help you," said Brac.

"No, no, no. When you fall, you have to pick yourself back up," said the G.O.A.T. "The last person to give me a fight like that was your father years ago, but we fought all the way to the top of the mountain. And then I knocked him off. But that darn man, he came back a year later."

Brac couldn't resist asking, "And he beat you?"

The G.O.A.T. looked at him and grinned, showing his gold teeth. "Let's just say, he got my consent."

Chapter 24

Ain't No Mountain High Enough

The rest of the way to the top of the mountain, Brac rode Mel, which was the G.O.A.T.'s real name. "I bet you can tell me a lot about the Arial World, Mel!" said Brac.

"Well, I've only been living for a couple hundred years, ya know," he said. "When I told you your father created me, I was actually brought back from my slumber by him. He was a knucklehead just like you." He lifted his leg, motioning toward the bracelets. "He had those same exact metals on when he interrupted my sleep. Haven't you noticed all the dents and dings on them?"

Brac looked and realized that they were pretty beat up.

"So you were asleep?" Brac asked.

"Yes, I needed my rest. No one else was worthy of my training, so I had decided to take a break from being a big bad furball." He chuckled, nudging Brac with his leg. "Knocking them off the mountain and stuff was tiring."

Brac wondered about the others that had come before him and asked, "Well, do you know how many people you've fought?"

"Hmm, thousands. I've been all over the universe, kid. There's nothing I haven't seen."

Brac was astounded. "That's a lot of people, Mel!"

"I know, but you and your father are two of the few who gave me problems." Side-stepping a rock in his path, Mel added, "Oh, and a guy named Vincitor, very dark and serious guy. He never smiled, not even once."

"Vincitor, you say. Hmph, how did he end up here in the Arial World?"

Mel shook his head. "I don't know, but that guy was creepy!"

"Well, he's in the first world now, and that's why I'm here," said Brac.

"They sent a child here to defeat Vincitor," Mel said with disbelief. "You must be a mighty special kid. Or all of you are just crazy."

"Was Vincitor strong?" asked Brac.

"He gave me a hard time. He was very strong, and from the looks of it, he was around your age!"

Brac was taken aback by what he said. "*My* age!?" He didn't want to show it, but that worried him a bit.

"Yes—your age, if not younger."

"So, did he beat you? Or did he put up a good enough fight to get your consent?" asked Brac.

Mel took a deep breath. "To be honest with you, that kid was so, so… he just had an aura that was completely menacing, and his strength was… it was… different. To be honest, I've been feeling something similar to it. Not as powerful, but the feeling's the same."

"Well, I'll just have to see for myself. I've come too far to back down," said Brac as he clenched his fist. "But do you mind me asking, what's at the top of the mountain?"

"What's up there varies by person, but it's always what they desire. When we make it up there, I'll leave. The rest is up to you because this is your journey. I was just a catalyst. You can't do everything on your own, kid."

When they were almost to the top, they had to make their way through thick clouds covering the peak of the mountain. "You can tell this is a sign of secrecy," Mel said. "There are no shortcuts. Even if you try to fly, it will not allow you to reach the top. The only way up is to start from the bottom. The mountain has to know you, it has to feel you! In some way, it even wants you to feel it. You have to earn what it has waiting for you."

Brac understood clearly.

"Okay," said Mel. "The rest is up to you."

Brac looked back at Mel and nodded his head, then continued through the clouds.

Chapter 25

You Create Your Own Destiny

The closer Brac got to the peak, the thinner the clouds got, but he still couldn't see very much; only his next step was visible. "How much longer will it take?" he said. "This is so nerve-racking. I don't have a clue what will happen." He was very anxious to see what was waiting for him.

He took a few more steps, then the ground fell away beneath him. Thanks to training, his reflexes were superb. When he caught himself, he grunted and said, "That was a nose breaker."

When he looked up, he found no great destiny, just a glass of clear liquid. "What?" he said as he picked himself up. "Water! My destiny is water!" It made no sense to him. "All of this for a glass of water!" He was about to throw it. "I didn't wish for this!" he shouted as he cocked back to sling the diamond glass down the mountain. But before he could build his momentum to pitch it—

"Aren't you thirsty?" came the voice of a woman from behind him. "That is some of the purest water in the universe," she said. "I believe you might want to cherish it rather than disrespect it."

When he turned around, he couldn't believe what he saw. His eyes bulged when he saw that same black ball of light that had started him on his journey: his clair. "You've done very well, Brac Guider!"

The look on Brac's face read, *What the hell*? "You can talk?" he said with disbelief.

"Well, of course," she said. "I just wanted to see how far you would go by using your own intuition."

She was right: everything that had happened, Brac had made his own decisions toward it.

"Correct," she said.

"My desire is to continue my journey. No matter what!"

"Before we take the next step, I need to explain something to you."

Brac was all ears.

"I am something called a Guider," she said.

"Like my last name?"

"Well, that part you will soon learn, but I am here to help and protect you. You are not dead, but you are in between life and death! That very seldom happens. With that being said, I had to detach myself from within you so I could use our full power to direct you through dimensions and so you could see and follow me. But it was up to you to make the decisions to do so," she said. "If you were fully dead, I would still be inside of you."

Brac thought back to his uncle's planet. "Well, on my uncle's planet, they had a lot of Guiders there, but they weren't occupied with anyone."

"Aimless Guiders are forever waiting for their hosts. Those hosts might be stuck in another dimension or might have outright rejected them. Like the people you first saw when you met Shakoora, they wanted to be at peace, plant flowers, lay in the sun, and be normal. They denied their destinies and true nature."

She broke down the bare essentials of life to him. On the mountain that day, he learned what even the oldest people in the first world would never know unless they'd experienced life in the Arial World. It was somehow the real world. The first world was like a matrix.

Chapter 26

Another Day

"Shakoora, you've been mighty quiet lately," said Tunne.

Shakoora took a deep breath. "I've just been wondering about—" She stopped.

"About Brac. I know how you feel, honey," said Tunne. "I felt the same way about your father. He was back and forth for some time, training to become the man he is today. He had to make sacrifices not just for me, but for the whole universe, and now Brac is doing the same. You have to keep in mind that he is a very strong young man, and it's vice versa with you. But you've never been in the first world, and he has been there all his life. Now he can end the tragedy he has been living in before it spreads."

That made Shakoora feel better. She knew Brac was gone for the better, but every day, she dwelled on the fact that he wasn't there. *Where could he be? What was he doing? And when will he return?* She realized that he was the savior, not just for his world, but for every world that existed. He truly reminded her of her father, and his progress was well known all around the Arial World. "You know what, Mama, you're right. He will be back, and stronger than ever." She smiled at her mother, and Tunne smiled back at her.

"Sweetheart, at the end of the day, everything will be all right."

Then there was a booming knock on the door. They both looked toward the sound, and then each other.

"I'll get it," said Shakoora. When she opened the door, she was shocked to see her father. "Daddy!"

The house grew three times bigger with the help of Tunne's magic, letting Bilge step inside. "Hey there," he said with his smooth, deep voice.

"Bilge," said Tunne, "come in. I know you're hungry, and the food's just about done."

"Well, don't mind if I do. I just finished arranging a planet in the fifth dimension. So, how is everything going with you two?" he asked.

They both grew quiet.

"Well, everything's been good this way," said Shakoora. "But we haven't talked to Brac since he left."

"Well, I have some news for you."

Shakoora got excited internally but hid it externally.

"There's a big threat coming across the universe, and all of the worlds are in danger," he said. "Vincitor has unleashed an energy that is very dangerous, and it's getting stronger day by day. It will take form shortly and become tangible. This is the biggest problem we've had in centuries."

"Well, how long do we actually have?" Still not getting any detail on Brac deeply bothered Shakoora, but she didn't show it.

"To be honest," said Bilge, "six months tops. Everyone needs to train. This force is ancestral." Then he added, "The time for peace is over; it is time for war." He smashed his fist on the solid wooden table. "I hate to do this, but I will need the both of you to help. And I'll need—"

"Me!" came a voice from behind.

The three of them startled and looked toward the door. Framed in the doorway was a dirty, muscular young man with long hair and a smile that could brighten up even Vincitor's day.

"Miss me?" said Brac.

Chapter 27

Purpose

"It won't be long before I rule." Vincitor sat in a room devoid of light, but his blood-red eyes pierced the dense darkness. "I've been peaceful for a long time, waiting only for this moment!" He clenched his fist. "When I reign, I will slap the most high down and make him clean my boots. I will be the greatest man to ever live or die! They all will bow to my might!"

"Sire!" It was his black hawk, Halcon. The hawk had been in the family for centuries. Vincitor's great-great-grandfather had gotten Halcon from a magician in order to stalk the rebels he'd been fighting, and the bird had been with the Vincitor line ever since.

"What is it, Halcon?" He snapped his fingers, and the room lit up with fire that engulfed the walls, but they did not burn.

Halcon landed on his forearm. "I was flying toward Colossus 'cause I haven't been that way in a while, and I sensed a very strange thing!" he shouted.

"What do you mean by 'a very strange thing'?" asked Vincitor.

"It was just weird, like something was there, but it wasn't there!"

Vincitor thought the bird was going mad. "Halcon, stop the antics."

Halcon pleaded his case. "I'm telling you the truth! Since you don't believe me, I'm going to go back and show you!" He hurried off to prove his case. The hawk's magic was perfectly suited for reconnaissance; if necessary, Vincitor could look through his eyes and see what he saw.

"He thinks I'm fibbing, huh? I'm going to find out who that was. Their power level was sky high. King Vincitor won't be pleased knowing there's another out there strong as he. Sire will be quite upset," he said. "Now let's see here, hmm. I was right about here when I felt it… there we go!" He swooped down and landed on a tree limb that hung in front of a cave entrance. "It's coming from in there." He glided down and peeped into the dark cave. Colossus was roaring behind him, plummeting into the plunge pool and creating a cloud of mist around the cave. He hopped off the tree with intent to go in.

As he drew near, his feathers ruffled with static. He quickly pulled back. "A shield," he said. An electric shield blocked the cave entrance. "Well, why is this here? He thinks I'm lying, huh? I'm going to show Master Vincitor!" Before he got a chance to hop up and take off, his legs were held by a strong grip. "What the heck?" He looked back to see none other than—"Artiest!"

"What are you doing here?" Halcon shouted. "And how did you get so strong?" Halcon wasn't a weakling, either; he could lift a full-grown man miles into the air before dropping him to his untimely death.

Artiest did not budge. "No more flying today, buddy," he said. With a crack, he broke both of Halcon's legs as if they were nothing more than dry twigs.

"You stupid man!" he yelled.

"You little lackey." He bent the hawk's head toward the shield.

"What are you doing, fool?" he shouted. "King Vincitor will have your head for this, you hear me! Aaahhh!" he screamed.

"Well, looks like chicken's for dinner." Artiest walked through the cave entrance. He had a comfy space, and on the floor, wrapped up, was Brac's lifeless body. "I know what's next," he said to the unmoving Brac. "But don't worry, I'll protect you if it takes my life!" He was dead serious; he knew Vincitor was coming, and he was prepared mentally and physically.

***

Halcon hadn't yet returned, and all attempts to see through the bird's eyes only resulted in darkness. As Vincitor moved through his castle, he could only think of what Halcon had been blabbing about the day before: the strange force by Colossus. "I wonder what he was talking about." He began to worry about the family jewel and grew so worried he decided to go and look for Halcon himself. "If something has happened to my bird, I will kill whoever did it!"

People were staring and saying, "Is that the king?" Everyone began to bow, some even pulling their children down, making them bow. He heard whispers but ignored them. He never really was seen by the people, but things change.

No one can be strong enough to kill Halcon, he thought to himself, having no idea where his family's treasure could be. The main thing was that he hadn't left the castle for a long time. It had always been in darkness, always in thought. He only talked to Halcon. He had no family or friends. He let it all die for power—he wanted everything to himself. He had so many scars and had caused so many.

***

"Hmph!" Artiest jumped up out of his sleep. "He's coming." So he began to prepare, hiding Brac's body and making sure he was untraceable. Artiest needed to double the strength of the shield so Vincitor could not sense anything within. To keep Brac's body preserved, he had left a little energy in it. But that little bit of energy was noticeable, especially to someone as strong as Vincitor. After he secured everything, he began to make his way to the top of Colossus, planning to beat Vincitor there. His plan was to lead him away from Brac. No one could know that he was neither completely dead nor alive.

This is it, he said to himself. It's my turn to play my part. Just like our father, I have to sacrifice for the better. He made it to the top and stood there, staring at the dark, dense forest. He's almost here.

"So, it was you that Halcon sensed!" cried that terrible voice, but it did not shake Artiest one bit.

He smirked. "I always hated that bird," he said. "I should have killed it years ago."

When he mentioned that, the look on Vincitor's face became murderous, soulless. "You killed my bird!" he screamed. "Now you will die!"

"Yeah, you deserve to die also! You murderous, lying sack of crap!" said Artiest. "You lied about everything, you self-serving lunatic. My mother, my father, my village, and my life! You stole my life!"

As the two faced off, they simultaneously dropped into a low pose, each ready for the other to make a move.

"I made you strong. Your father was weak, and your mother, she didn't know how to run her village, so it had no reason to exist. After your grandfather and grandmother died, that village was supposed to die also."

They were at each other's throats. The truth was spoken, and their temperatures were rising. "Well, if I could take you down, I'd be doing the world a favor."

Artiest charged at Vincitor, and Vincitor charged as well. They met with a huge headbutt. They clashed like two rams, pushing each other with so much force that the ground began to crack. They began to grapple with their foreheads still pressed together, neither backing down.

"I've gotten much stronger, Diyar, so you won't be able to brush me aside so easily!" Artiest was holding his own.

Vincitor met Artiest's eyes and smiled. "You think you're actually doing something, boy? This is to test your might," he said. "And it is weak!" He smashed his foot into Artiest's chest, sending him flying! But Vincitor was fast. Artiest was still stumbling backward when Vincitor grabbed him by his hair with one hand and drove the other into his gut. "Look at you, the spawn of a pathetic bloodline."

Artiest grabbed Vincitor's wrist and said, "Shut up!"

He kicked Vincitor hard upside the head. Vincitor let go of his wrist, and Artiest followed it up with another kick to Vincitor's side and then a right hook to the ear, the latter of which sent Vincitor crashing into a tree. Leaves rained down on him with the impact.

"Hmm, this will be quite interesting," he said as he wiped the black blood from his mouth. "Father versus son, for the big one!"

They both rushed in and fell into a melee, hitting one another with ferocious blows, but neither one copped out. They both stumbled back. Artiest quickly tried to jump back in, and he landed a hit right to Vincitor's mouth, then to his eye, and one giant punch to his jaw. As Vincitor fell to one knee, Artiest kicked him so hard in the head that his whole body lifted off the ground and twisted through the air. Vincitor crashed into another tree—this time breaking it. Birds fled; animals ran.

"I remember being by your side." Artiest's eyes were damp. "You were all the family I had; I had nothing without you," he said. "I met my father and tried to kill him. What I've been training for my whole life was all based on a lie!"

Vincitor staggered to his feet, laughing softly.

"What do you find so funny, you *monster*?" Tears fell down Artiest's face.

"How I set you all up, and you never even had a clue. You've been training for revenge—for something that never even happened. I got you to the point where you wanted to kill your father, my rebellious enemy, who got my daughter pregnant and turned her against me." As he continued to talk, his eyes began to get redder and redder, and his skin grayer and grayer.

Artiest had never seen that side of Vincitor before.

"You think I give a damn about turning a man's son against him after he turned my precious princess against me? My heart had turned cold long before then, and now it's frozen solid! Get ready to meet your foolish father and ancestors!"

Artiest felt Vincitor's power increasing. "How did he even get this strong?" he said aloud.

"My hate, it drives me, makes me strong. You have just signed your death warrant, boy!"

Artiest knew he was in trouble—the sky was turning colors. It was a swirl of red and gray. Lightning and thunder crackled across the sky, scattering the remaining animals.

"If I die, then I die! This is my final strike whether it kills you or not!" Artiest shouted.

As Artiest ran toward Vincitor, everything fell silent. He drew back his arm like a bow, and so did Vincitor. They both screamed a wordless battle cry into the silence.

Chapter 28

The Universal Book

"Brac!" Shakoora cheered, greeting him with an inescapable hug. "We were just talking about you!" She squeezed him tight.

"Well, I've been thinking about you all too," he said.

"You made it just in time, son," said Tunne. "The food's just finished."

His smile grew wide enough that his eyes all but disappeared in his joy. "That's great. I'm starving! Mr. Bilge, how are you?" he asked.

"Well, I'm doing just grand! How was your training?"

Brac looked relaxed and unbothered. "Training taught me life is eternal, so there's no need to seek knowledge because it's never-ending, so it's like it doesn't even exist. Knowledge is like a void. It's there, but it's not there. It's not like finding treasure because when you find a treasure, it's yours. Knowledge is not something you can obtain for yourself because someone always knows what you think, yet no one knows. It's nothing personal. It's universal and meant to be shared. This understanding is what I'll take with me into the battlefield."

Those were his words, and he could tell by the expressions of the room around him that he'd said something meaningful. "Hmm, you were taught well, my boy," said the Grand Bilge. "I can tell that you've reached an unimaginable level of power." He nodded once at Brac, and Brac nodded back.

"Come, let's eat!" said Tunne.

"Well, I have some news for you, Brac," said Bilge. "There is a great threat coming."

"I already know," Brac replied. "I'm here for one thing, and that's to become great enough to save my world from Vincitor." He paused. "Now I have to help save the entire universe."

Everyone just stared in silence.

"I can't wait!" He was utterly excited.

"We don't know exactly what Vincitor is trying to do, but we know it's serious. The power he's tampering with belongs to one of the oldest beings to ever exist."

"Wow! Who is he?" Brac asked.

"You mean she."

Brac was surprised. "She! It's a woman?" Why, he couldn't believe it.

"Well, what's wrong with it being a lady?" Shakoora folded her arms and turned her head away from Brac in disgust.

"Oh, nothing! Umm, I just thought that it would be a—a man." Brac blushed while scratching his head.

"Hmph," she replied.

"Shakoora, he just assumed it was a man; you know how men are," said Tunne.

"Whatever!" she snapped.

"Anyhow," said Bilge, "we all need to be prepared—every world needs to. We don't know where it'll strike first."

"But didn't you say that Vincitor called on it, so it'll be in the first world, right?" asked Brac.

"No, this power can travel through dimensions at the speed of light. It just wants a host, and Vincitor seems to be the perfect one to harness its power and not burst into oblivion."

Brac was still confused. "But how do you all know it wants Vincitor?"

"A little while before you children were born, Vincitor used a powerful magic to get his hands on *The Book of a Million Pages*. It's said to carry the story of forever and a day, and it supposedly tells the truth about the universe. I have heard of it, but never did I think it existed."

"Wow, so you mean to tell me he sat up there and read a million pages?"

Bilge looked at Brac. "A million and one," he corrected.

"Man, so he basically deserves that power, huh? There's no way I could have done that," said Brac.

The door suddenly shook with three booming knocks, and everyone turned toward it.

"I'll get it." Brac walked to it and pulled. The door squeaked open. To his surprise, it was none other than Artiest. "Artiest!"

Both stared each other in the eyes, neither one blinking.

"To be honest, I don't know what to say," said Brac.

"You can start when—and where—ever you want. I'll wait."

Brac was lost for words. After all the training and preparation, nothing could have readied him for that encounter. "What happened to you?"

"I've been protecting your body since you've been gone. And I knew the time would come when I'd have to put my life up for yours. I gave my word, so I had to play my part."

Brac walked up to him with his arms spread out. "Thank you." He gave his brother a great hug out of love and respect.

"I wanted to fight alongside you, but it looks like I'll have to watch from a distance," said Artiest.

"Don't you worry. I'll get him for you—for everybody! It's only a matter of time." He clenched his fist.

"Brac!" shouted Bilge. "Your brother is welcome to feast."

"Come on," said Brac. "Join us."

No one knew how hungry Artiest really was—that is, until his stomach growled.

"Well, I hope you like gumbo, Artiest!" said Tunne.

They all laughed.

"I'll eat anything right about now," he said while blushing hard.

Tunne brought the rice and the huge pot to the table. "Go ahead," she said. "You can eat however much you want—you need your strength."

They both looked at each other, then at her. "Thank you, Mrs. Tunne!" And they dug in, eating like wild dogs.

"That was delicious!" said Artiest.

"The best!" followed Brac.

"So, back to business," Bilge stated. "We were discussing *The Book of a Million Pages*, Artiest."

"Why, I've heard of it but always looked at it as a myth. Vincitor was the one to always mention it," he said.

"Well, it isn't a myth. It's very real, and Vincitor has it."

Artiest's eyes bulged. "But if he has that book, then that means all of the things he said—I mean, the power! I just fought him, but I felt like he was holding back for some reason. The final punch he landed nearly knocked my head off. He hit me so hard I flew and fell straight down Colossus!" he said. "What are we to do now? Brac, I'm warning you, he has something none of us have. He's cold, really cold. And now since he has that book—"

"I don't care about that!" Brac shouted, then looked Artiest dead in the eyes. "I am not afraid of anything!" he said fiercely.

Everyone just stood there. No one had expected that from Brac.

"I—I'm sorry about that," Brac said sincerely. "I just—I just don't want to hear anything negative."

Artiest smiled and patted him on the shoulder. "Sorry about that, Brac. You're right, but what I said was only the truth. Vincitor told me stories about that book; it's very powerful. I never thought he would actually find it. The universe is in great danger," he said, but with a smirk. "But you, Brac, you have the power to change things. It is your destiny."

Chapter 29

The Rising Sun

A knocking interrupted their conversation, rattling the door's hinges. They all looked back.

"Who is it this time?" Shakoora went to open the door.

"Arbre!" Brac said with surprise and excitement.

"Arbre?" Shakoora repeated.

"Brac!" Arbre ran and gave Brac a huge hug and a little peck on the cheek.

Shakoora seemed displeased by that turn of events. "Hey, don't just walk into people's home without greeting anyone!" she scolded, her brow furrowed.

Arbre ignored Shakoora's every word. "Oh, Brac, I've been so worried about you!"

Shakoora glared. "Why, you little—"

Bilge, Tunne, and Artiest had to grab Shakoora before she lunged at Arbre.

"Um, Arbre, you should introduce yourself," Brac said.

"Oh," she said and turned around. "Hi, everyone, my name's Arbre. I'm Brac's good friend!"

"Hello, Arbre!" they all said—well, except Shakoora, that is.

"Little jerk." She shook off the people holding her back. "Let me go."

"How did you get here, Arbre?" asked Brac.

"Your father sent me. He said, 'Go with Brac. He'll need some company.' And I got sent here!" she said.

"Well, I guess that's cool. You were my catalyst." They both smiled.

"All right, enough with the sweet talk. Brac, you have to get prepared to leave," Shakoora said, tired of the smiling from the two already.

"Okay, you ready, Arbre?" asked Brac.

"Of course," she said.

Everyone met up at the cave later that day, the same cave that Brac first entered in the beginning. They were preparing Brac for whatever might happen in the first world.

"Now," said Bilge, "you'll be going to Colossus. When you get there, you will wake in your body, but you'll have to keep your power level down. And when you want to communicate with one of us, just close your eyes and think about whoever it is. We'll be on standby!"

Brac gave him a nod.

"I made something for you." Tunne pulled out a brown palm-sized sack. "It's pure melaton, so if you feel hungry or you need a boost, take one a day, and only one!"

He nodded and gave her a hug. "Thank you, Mrs. Tunne."

Next was Shakoora. She looked like she wanted to kick him in the butt and say good riddance. But she actually began to cry. "Brac," she muttered, "be careful." She laid her head on his shoulder.

"If I have the power to do anything, I have the power to come back safe, right?" He wiped away her tears with his sleeve, then stepped away, back to Arbre. "Well, I guess it's time for us to go. Thank you all for helping me. I owe you more than I can give."

They all smiled.

"Ready?" He looked at Arbre, and she nodded her head.

When they entered the cave, the walls were pure white, but at the end, there was darkness. "I guess we have to go all the way down. This is kind of exciting," said Brac. "I haven't been to the first world in forever, but I know the first place I have to go." Brac knew he was going to shock everyone when he returned. The first stop was his village.

"I'm kind of nervous," said Arbre. "I mean, meeting your people and all."

"Oh, don't worry—that part will be a breeze, but we have a whole universe to save. They must really have faith in us, huh?" Brac said with a smile.

They made it to the end of the cave, but before they could leave, Brac's vision swam. He broke out in a sweat as images passed before his eyes: starving people being beaten, the land being stripped of life by slaves, and then, watching everything, the dark, cold eyes of a monster.

"Brac, are you okay?" said Arbre.

He came back to himself, fury coiling in his stomach as he stared at the white light in front him. Those had been his people—his people and his world—all being mistreated by Vincitor. "Come on."

Arbre looked at him, then the passageway. They both walked in and vanished.

His eyes opened, and everything was a blur. His vision came and went. When he realized where he was, he sat up. His body was so stiff that it sounded like a board breaking in half. "Ouch! So this is what happens when you lie down for a couple of years, good god!" He took his time to stand up. He actually had no choice in the matter. His body was so stiff that he could barely bend his legs. "Why do I still have this weak, frail body?" He closed his eyes and thought about Bilge. "Mr. Bilge, come in!" he called out in his mind.

"Yes?" answered Bilge. "What is it?"

"What's up with this body?" he asked.

"It'll take some time to catch up. As you continue on, your body will adjust, don't worry."

He agreed as he struggled to rise, stumbling a little when he was on his feet. Leaning on the cave helped him make it to the fake wall his brother told him about, and from there, he limped his way out. When he passed through the shield, Arbre was right there, staring at Colossus.

"It's huge!" She looked back at him. "Wow, you look like you just came back from the dead!"

"Well, I kinda did," he said. "Anyway, Bilge said my body needs some time to change. So I guess we'll be here for a while." And he sat—well, more like fell—down.

"Are you sure it's safe to be out here in the open like this?" asked Arbre.

"Yeah, we'll be just fine. It won't be long until my body develops. I don't want to be a burden to you." So they waited.

Chapter 30

Nada

Brac felt his body getting a bit stronger. His form was taking shape, and he felt a little livelier than before. "I can feel it. I'm starting to feel alive." He could sort of clench his fist, but his body still felt limp.

"You'll be fine," she said. "I just hope we can stay discreet until you're fully healed. Wouldn't want Vincitor to pop up." She smiled, but Brac knew that was the honest truth.

"So you haven't been feeling a little strange since we've been here?" she asked.

"To be honest, I've been feeling strange since we were in the cave, like a weird energy was around or something, but being here is like being surrounded by negativity, so maybe that's what it is."

She looked off into the sky with wondering eyes. "Something's out there," she said, "and it's coming."

The sun was high in the sky, but the clouds around it were so heavy it made no difference. That was how things were in the first world: dark, gloomy, and soaked in misery. But beneath it, Brac could sense the energy—malevolent and coming closer. "I'm feeling it. I'm going to see if I can stand."

Arbre tried to help.

"No, I have to do this. Thanks, though."

She stepped back but was visibly ready to catch him. "You got it, Brac," she said softly.

He grunted but was making his way up. "Ah!" He did it. "Okay, now to walk." He almost felt like a baby as he put one unsteady foot in front of the other.

"There you go!" she said.

He took a couple steps and collapsed.

"You okay?" She ran to him.

"Yes, I'm fine. Just a little while longer."

They both sat down, but she jumped right back up. "Oh no!" she said. "Do you feel that?"

He did indeed, but his reaction time was a little off. "Vincitor," he said.

A woman's voice, loud and cruel, echoed around them. "You dare mistake me for your mortal ruler! If I had my body, I would destroy you both!"

They were a bit shaken. She was a dark, shapeless figure with pure-white eyes. Her form swirled around them; smoke crept across the ground, and everything it touched wilted.

"I sense the same kind of energy coming from you—the smell of your blood resembles his too. But your heart, your heart isn't cold as his. You aren't what I'm looking for." Then she turned into a figure, taking the shape of a perfect woman and walking up to Brac. "You seem to be a spawn of his." She rubbed his cheek. "Hmm, son. No—grandson!"

Brac began to get annoyed. "*Don't you touch me*!" he shouted as he sprang up.

The cloth wrapping him shifted as his body returned to its Arial World state, and upon glancing over at him, Arbre saw a good deal more than she meant to see.

"You dare stand up to me!" Nada was furious. "I'll destroy you! I'll destroy you all!" She gave an ear-splitting scream and darted off.

Brac turned around. "Are you okay?" he asked, not noticing he was missing something. "Why are you covering your eyes?" He looked down. "Oh crap!" He jumped in the river to cover up.

"I'll make you some clothes. Just stay right there." Arbre grabbed a piece of thread from her shirt, then another. She blew on them, and they got longer and started to thread together.

"Wow, you have the magic touch, huh?" he said.

"Just put these on, please." She blushed as she threw them at him.

"That was crazy, but I wonder what Vincitor's planning on doing with her. She seems like the type to not let anybody rule her," he said. "If that's his plan, then he might as well give up."

Arbre looked at Brac and shrugged her shoulders. "Well, Brac, she does need a physical body to use her powers, so I believe she's going to give them to Vincitor, or maybe they might do some type of thing where they both share the same body."

"Well, we'll find out sooner or later. But first things first, we have to go to my village," he said. "I have to see how everyone's doing."

Arbre grinned and offered him her arm, visibly trying to shake off their frightening encounter. "Well, what are we waiting for? Let's go."

Chapter 31

Black on Black

The torches of Vincitor's throne room ignited, cutting through the darkness and announcing Nada's arrival. "You've finally made it," he said. He felt her power.

"You called?" Then, out of nowhere, she showed herself. She was a shadow in the shape of a woman, her gaze black with an immeasurable ferocity. Something about her made it clear that she would be more likely to bite a man's head off before she would kneel before him.

"The most powerful woman in the universe: Nada!" he said, and then stepped off his throne. "I called, and you came." His breath caught when he felt the immense energy coming from her. Her power was unimaginable, like something out of a dream. Her aura was akin to that of a thunderstorm or a tsunami—a perfect force of nature.

"I'm here for you. Whatever you want, I will give it to you!" she said.

"I want you to become one with me! I want your power. I want to rule *everything*! Everything I see, every piece of land I walk on, and everything that breathes and dies!" His greed was at an all-time high. He wanted her power badly. "I want to be the ultimate conqueror! No one shall challenge or be greater than I! Not even the *gods* themselves!" He knew that man didn't hold the most dominant power, and that was why he'd called on her.

"You know, I've been looking for the perfect man who can handle my power. You seem quite strong, with a heart cold as ice. If I give you my strength, will you be able to handle it?" she asked.

"I can handle anything dead or alive," he said, "so try me."

She walked up to him and put her hands on his armored chest. "You know, I don't even remember the last time I did this." She leaned down and pressed her cold, smoky lips to his.

The flames roared. Vincitor's skin came alive with black veins. The mark of Nada's mouth against his went darker still. Nada cackled as the darkness consumed him, and her laughter tore through the castle walls. Then, she burst into millions of particles and surrounded Vincitor.

"Come to me!" he shouted. She darted into every part of his body, and he flew through the castle ceiling into the sky. He stopped and stared down at his kingdom, feeling like everything and everyone was below him. It was his world, and it would soon be his universe.

Chapter 32

Warrior's Playground

"Did you feel that?" asked Brac.

"Yeah, it's like two different energies suddenly became intertwined. Do you think—?" She stopped herself before she could form the question. She didn't need to finish—he knew what she meant.

"It's done!" he said.

Arbre nodded her head in agreement.

"Look, we need to get to my village. I feel like things are about to get real and more dangerous very soon!"

They dashed off through the woods. Neither one of them could slow down even for a moment; they knew there was no time.

When they made it to Brac's village, it was surrounded by a giant wall of rocks. "Wow, looks like they did a little renovating." The wall was clearly higher than fifteen feet.

"So why don't we just climb?" said Arbre.

"We can. I just hope they don't think we're the enemies!"

They climbed up in silence, Brac desperate to see something of his home again. But when they reached the top and Brac stared down into the space within the wall, he found it empty of life. There were no people or animals. Everything was deadly still. "What's going on?" He was taken aback that nothing was there. "I know this is where my village was. I don't understand." He was utterly confused. "This doesn't make any sense…" He remembered his way around very well, but where was everyone? Dead?

"Maybe after all that happened, they decided to move," said Arbre.

"I don't know, but I have to find them! But I don't know the first place to look."

"How about here?"

A fist came crashing into Brac's chin, knocking him for a loop.

When his vision cleared, he looked around for Arbre. In a panicked state, he shouted, "Arbre? Arbre? What was that?"

He looked over and saw Arbre and his mother.

"Brac! Are you okay?" said Arbre.

"He's fine—I only got him in the chin. If I'd hit him in the nose, then he wouldn't be."

His eyes grew wide. "Mama!" he murmured.

"Yep, that's me. Your friend told me everything. You are a brave young man, baby."

He felt almost like a child, tears welling up in his eyes. "I missed you so much!" Vision blurry, he ran to hug her.

She slapped him and grabbed him by the scruff of his neck. "You know how much you all hurt me, you and your father? Do you?"

Brac just stared at her.

"It's okay, Mrs. Guider," said Arbre. "They didn't mean to hurt you, but it had to be done. We've been through so much, and now we have to save the universe. Just please cut him some slack."

She slowly released him. "For years I have been traumatized by your father's death, and to find out that you've been trapped between life and death—I don't know what else is being hidden! And the whole time your father set all of this up without telling me *anything*! I moved the village after you were both gone." Her voice was pained. "I had to be strong for our people and find a safer place to live, but I couldn't leave you behind. Somehow, I just knew that you would be back, Brac. I've been here ever since."

"Mom, I didn't know a thing about any of this until I went to the Arial World. But I know it was all worth it! I just know it!" he said confidently.

"It will never be worth the years I spent without the two of you." His mother's voice was soft and bitter. She looked older, Brac realized, like she had been aged by the weight of her grief and leadership.

"Well, that's about to change," said Brac.

"What do you mean?" his mother asked.

"He read The Book of a Million Pages."

She gasped. "What? But I thought that was just a myth!" she said with disbelief.

"Far from it—the book has a chapter that tells you about some of the most powerful beings to ever exist. And how to call on them. One of those spirits is here as we speak," he said.

"What?" She couldn't believe what she was hearing.

"We had an encounter with her before we came here. Luckily, Brac ran her off," said Arbre.

"You must be something else, huh, son?" Adore proudly said, making him blush.

"She was looking for Vincitor. And, just a while ago, we felt a strange energy—it gave me chills," said Arbre.

"It's about to be a battle. I can feel it. He's going to come here. He doesn't want anyone to be stronger than him, and I know that Nada will tell him about her running into us," he said.

It was only a matter of time before the future of the universe was in their hands. Her hand pressed to her chest in horror, his mother looked like she couldn't believe what she was hearing.

Chapter 33

The Savior

They all had gotten some well-needed rest. Despite the fact that Vincitor could have appeared at any moment, even Brac slept like a baby. It was only a matter of time before the future of the universe was in their hands. Brac alone would have to shoulder the brunt of it, as everyone had deemed him their savior, but he was glad to know he wouldn't have to do it alone. Brac Guider was ready for war! He lay there in his hut longer than everyone else, thinking about how he had come from nothing to become the man who would save the universe. "It's been a long year, huh? I'm supposed to be the savior of all humankind. I've died and come back, I've learned that everything I knew was a lie, I've fought a magical goat, I've met new people—and now I'm attempting to battle one of the most powerful beings to ever live." He then grew quiet. "It feels so unreal—I mean—to be this person that I've become." Looking back on everything that he had been through gave him a burst of confidence. "If I can make it through all of those burdens, then what makes this so difficult?" he said. "I'm Brac Guider. I've made a name for myself to all that matter. I won't fold! Vincitor, you better be prepared."

"Brac!" called a young child. "Wake up, there are some strange people out here for you!" Then the boy struck off.

Brac thought he was dreaming. Crazy thing was, it was him. That boy with the ragged shirt and nappy hair woke him, then vanished.

He got up slowly to keep calm—jumping up would just throw off his focus and make his blood boil. "Strange people, huh?" he said calmly. "Must be time." There was only one person on his mind, but he was calm, very calm.

He stretched before walking out of his hut, ready for his calling. He moved toward the door and said, "At the end of the day, everything will be all right." He stepped out, and there he saw everyone gathered in a huge circle. He walked up, and they parted. They all were still there. Awaiting a savior, his mother had kept them alive and also kept them with faith.

"Well, hello, Brac!"

It was an old man, with many others crowded around him. "H-hello?" He had no idea who those people were.

"We've been waiting to see you!"

"To see me? What do you mean?" Brac was confused. He didn't know where everyone had come from.

"Your mother," said the old man. "She said you would return; she's been singing the same song since you fell down Colossus. But you've really returned. A true savior!"

"I'm sorry, but I just don't understand. No one knew about this but certain people. You're all welcome to stay, but what's about to happen is going to be dangerous. I'd feel guilty if anyone were to get hurt," said Brac.

"Oh, don't worry about us. We'll be perfectly fine. We're a family of fighters," said the old man, adding a smile. "We're actually here to help."

"Help! No, no, *no*! I don't want you to help! This is too dangerous for you all—it's dangerous for anyone! Even me!" Brac preached.

The old man did not listen. "Look, son, I'll tell you what," he said. "How about me and you have a little sparring match, and if I impress you, we all can give a helping hand if needed?"

He was the kindest-looking old man. "I-I can't do it," said Brac.

"Just let me show you. You won't be disappointed," he said, still smiling.

Brac took a deep breath. "Okay. Come on!"

Brac fell back into a fighting stance. Before he could even blink, the old man was behind him. Brac leaped away as the old man attempted to sweep his legs from underneath him. He tried to counter with a kick to the head.

The old man blocked him easily, then sent a punch right to Brac's gut. His moves were fast enough that Brac barely managed to block them in time. They were in an impasse: the old man struggled to land that hit, and Brac held him back. "You're strong, old man!" he said. "But not strong enough!"

Brac pushed off, and then chuckled. "Okay. You are what you say you are." Brac was truly astounded by his performance. "Where did you all come from?" he asked.

"We've been here for a long time. Why, I was here the day you were born. This world can be saved—your mother's been preaching that! She said one day when she visited Colossus, a man came and told her of a prophet, which was you. He's what they call an alchemist."

Brac had never heard of an alchemist before. "An alchemist? Arbre," said Brac, "do you have any idea what he's talking about?"

She put on a big smile and said, "Yes, my father was an alchemist! He was greatly praised for many things back at home!"

Brac didn't want anyone to get hurt, but having backup did sound good. It wasn't like there was a rulebook on how to save the world, after all. "Okay. We can do the team thing. Just don't try to take him yourselves," he said. "Let me start it off."

Nobody knew when Vincitor would appear. No one even knew where he was. Word had come from the city where Vincitor had made his stronghold. The castle had been abandoned.

Chapter 34

A Legend is Born!

The change was upon them almost instantly. Above their heads, the sky grew darker. Black clouds gathered, rumbling with approaching thunder. Around them, the air cooled rapidly, raising gooseflesh on bare skin. Terror oozed into the hearts of the people—Brac could see it on every face as the lighting flashed wildly above them.

"He's coming," said Brac. "I can feel him. His wickedness is flowing through the air. It's giving me chills." He knew one thing, and that was to keep his composure. If he didn't, then fear would creep up on him in an instant.

"Listen, all of you. Stay back, and do not come between us!" he shouted.

"But Brac, we can help!" Arbre pleaded.

"No, not with this one. I didn't know he was this strong!"

The wind howled around them. It was as if they were caught in the strength of a hurricane. With a roar of thunder, something dropped from the sky. The ground crumbled under the force of the impact, forming a crater in the middle of the village.

"Be afraid, mortals!" The deep voice rang out like thunder itself, and Vincitor came floating up from the crater. Spotting Adore, his mouth curved into a wicked grin. "My darling daughter, how have you been? How is your husband? Still dead?" He then let out a frantic laugh.

"How dare you mock my pain, you heartless monster. I am no daughter of yours!"

From the corner of his eye, Brac could see the way her fists were clenching.

"You're nothing more than a parasite, and everything you touch you drain of love." Her rage seemed to overpower her then, and she rushed her father with murderous intent, crying, "You worthless beast!"

Vincitor didn't move as his daughter hurtled toward him. He simply grinned. Adore had gotten close enough to land a hit, but he was faster. He would hit her first, shattering her skull, and her blow would never connect. But someone else intercepted his fist.

"Your fight is with me!" said Brac while clutching Vincitor's hand. "No one here has anything to do with this as far as I can see! You're mine!" His soul was in those words.

"Aren't you supposed to be dead?" asked Vincitor.

"There's a lot that you don't know, like how I'm going to get rid of you. I feel the same way about you that my mother does: being your grandson disgusts me," he said.

"I don't care about you, your mother, or your father," Vincitor said, then he quickly twisted free from Brac's grip and grabbed his wrist with great force. "I will destroy you all and start over. It sickens me to have such weaklings for spawn!" Then he pulled Brac close, snapping his wrist.

Brac shouted in pain.

"I'll kill you first—"

With a hideous crack, Brac headbutted him in the mouth. Vincitor's grip loosened, and Brac took the opportunity to punch him hard in the ribs before throwing a flurry of blows. Brac kept changing his targets—body, head, head, body—and followed them up with a roundhouse kick to the head. Vincitor's head snapped to one side, and Brac fell into a fighting stance.

"Did he just do that?" he heard his mother ask, her voice pitched high in shock. "Maybe—maybe we have a chance after all."

Vincitor cracked his neck and grew furious. "Now, boy, *let me show you true power*!" He raised his hands toward the sky, and instantly, a red mist began to seep from his body. "This is the true power of negativity: my power and that of Nada, the strongest being to ever exist! You cannot struggle, cannot escape—in fact, it will be easier on all of you to simply stand there and die!" he shouted as the ground shook beneath their feet.

"Everyone go! Get away from here!" shouted Brac.

"I don't care how strong he is! I'm not leaving you behind! That's cowardly!" said Arbre. "You can all go, but I'll stay."

"Arbre, why don't you listen?" he said.

"Because, Brac, you're my friend, and friends don't abandon one another!"

He looked back and smiled despite the sweat gathering on his forehead. "Well, you stay then! Mother, take everyone else as far as possible! Keep them safe!"

She nodded before turning away and shouting firm instructions at the straggling villagers to run.

"I'll kill you first, then all of them!" Vincitor flew at him, one hand wrapping around Brac's throat. "You will be going to the other world today, and this time, I'll make sure you're dead!"

Vincitor slammed him against a tree, choking him in a vice grip. "You're weak!" he declared.

To Brac's horror, Vincitor brought their faces together, close enough that Brac could see the darkness writhing under his skin and feel the cold breath against his cheek.

"Every world will be like this," Vincitor breathed into his ear, "and I will kill anyone who gets in my way."

Brac began to black out.

"I'm going to rule over all."

With a horrible crack, Brac felt the tree beneath him splinter.

"I will bring a new age to this world."

He squeezed harder. Black spots floated before Brac's eyes.

"All the people will be mine to command. The suns of every world will go dark."

But that was not the end…

Vincitor began to feel his hand being pushed back. "What?"

Brac had braced himself against the tree, countering Vincitor's chokehold as best he could by wrapping his hands around his grandfather's arm. As he struggled, he gritted out between his teeth, "You won't make it off this planet."

Vincitor's grip on his throat shifted, allowing him to gulp down fresh air.

"And I promise you that!"

Vincitor was mumbling to himself, staring at Brac as if he'd never seen him before. "This boy must have the strength of—no, he couldn't possibly! But he keeps pulling power from nowhere, just like her."

Brac grabbed Vincitor's wrist with both hands, turned his neck, and chomped down on his finger. Vincitor's mumbling cut off with a shriek of pain. "Ahh! You savage little degenerate!"

Brac stepped away from Vincitor, who stood there cradling his injured hand with an expression of disbelief. Pleased with the horror on his grandfather's face, Brac spat a glob of dark blood at the earth. "Hmph, I have enough of your crap in me already," he said with a smile. "When I'm done with you, I'm going to change this world, make it a better place—and anyone who stands in my way after you will be defeated!" Brac rushed Vincitor again before he could respond.

This time, it was full-fledged combat. They traded brutal blows faster than the human eye could see, but they were evenly matched on all fronts. The fight could have gone on forever.

"He fights just like his father," said Adore.

Brac dodged a kick by an inch, and they both stopped.

"How? How did you get so strong?" asked Vincitor.

"I accepted death, so fear has no place inside of me," he said.

"So you think this is it?" Vincitor asked, gesturing toward himself. "I hope you're not at your full power, boy, because if so, you're dead!"

Brac was giving it his all, so he decided to bluff. Maybe he could find a way to beat Vincitor, but if his grandfather wasn't using his full power yet, then exactly how strong was he? "I don't know about you, but I'm just getting warmed up," said Brac.

"Well, let me show you some real power!"

Brac didn't show any signs on the outside, but on the inside, his fear was taking over.

"Now!" A burst of energy exploded from Vincitor, but Brac had to keep his poker face, so in no type of way could he hesitate.

When the dust settled, Vincitor was radiating heat like the sun itself had been trapped within him. The very air shimmered in his presence. Red electricity was curling off his body with an audible crackling. Brac had never witnessed power like that. His father had never shown him anything so terrible.

"Scared?"

At the sound of the new voice, Brac looked around for the source. Then, he realized that the voice had been too clear to be present on the battlefield. It had been coming from inside him. "Who's there?" he said.

"You don't have to use your mouth, you know. Some things are better left unsaid—like the fear I can feel growing within you. You're doing a fine job of hiding it." Brac caught the voice.

"Father!" he realized.

"You catch on quickly, huh?" Brac Sr. said.

"Where are you?" Brac asked.

"I'm in the Arial World with Bilge, Tunne, Shakoora, and Artiest," he said. "I've actually been here for some time now. We have been watching the fight."

"So you all have been watching me the whole time?" he thought.

"Yes, and we knew you were getting discouraged, so we decided to give you a little advice."

That calmed Brac a little. "Okay, and what's that?" he asked.

"Remember what you went through to prepare for this moment—all of the things you've seen, all of the people you have met who put their faith in you. Your hard training. We knew you were the one, the one who would change things. Remember the mountaintop, and what you have inside of you! And oh yeah, *stop being a coward! You know what's on the line, huh? Everything! Now get your tail from between your legs and fight, dammit! That man has been enslaving that world for as long as I can remember, and you're just going to play around with him until he kills you, huh? Wake the hell up, Brac! You said you wanted to be great! Now prove it!*"

Arbre and Adore shouted his name. "Brac! Brac! Wake up! What are you doing?"

They were too late. With a boom like thunder, Vincitor struck him and sent him flying through a hut.

Vincitor laughed a little, looking almost surprised. "He must have been too frightened to dodge. What a pity." He then looked toward everyone else, but Arbre jumped to defend them. No one had left.

"Stay back, you creep!" she yelled. "Everyone huddle up close to me!"

Vincitor seemed unbothered by her magic and kept advancing. When he was close, he reached out a hand and flicked the shield lightly. It broke like glass and vanished. He grabbed Arbre by her shirt and stared her down menacingly. "Now it's your turn to die, you little witch!"

Then something smacked him across his head. When he looked back over his shoulder, he saw Adore wielding a broken tree branch. "Put her down, scum!" she shouted. "I'm not afraid of you!" Then she cracked him with it again, breaking the branch on his head.

He threw Arbre down as if she were nothing but a rag doll. Then, without pause, he punched Adore in the face, the impact against her skull sounding like a gunshot. The force slammed Adore into the ground, her face caved in and her eyes wide open and sightless. She did not move again.

"You monster!" shouted Arbre. And out of her hand appeared a sword. "I'll kill you for that!" She charged him with the sword in hand.

"How dare you challenge me!" He easily stopped the attack with two fingers and sent a lightning bolt through the sword, causing it to glow red hot. The shockwaves ran through her body, and she fell to the ground.

"Peasants don't deserve to live among kings nor gods. Now, all of you will perish. You're not even worth being enslaved. Your weakness should be decimated. I'm tired of you all breathing the same air as me," he snarled as he stalked toward the remaining villagers. "I'll enjoy wiping out the rebel scum from this entire universe, and only the superior beings shall rule it!" He grabbed hold of the first victim. "You may be the first to be vanquished." He drew back to knock the man's head off but stopped in mid-action. Someone was holding him by the shoulder.

"I'd like to see you try," they said softly.

"What the—!" When he looked back, he met Brac's furious stare. "You imbecile!" He dropped the man but still couldn't move. "Let me go, you thrall!" he shouted.

"You took over the minds and bodies of billions of people, and you think I'm going to listen to you. You never had mercy for anyone! You have slaughtered millions, turned our world dark, and murdered my parents! You don't deserve crap on a *plate*!" Brac shouted as he hit Vincitor straight in the nose with a right hook.

With a crack of bone, Vincitor went flying, and Brac flew after him. He was so fast that he caught Vincitor by the ankles and stopped him in midair, hurling him face-first into a boulder and breaking it.

"Get up," said Brac. "*Get up*!" He then grabbed Vincitor by his hair and picked him up. "You're pathetic. I thought no one could beat you. I thought you were a *god*!" He punched him in the gut. "You killed my people!" Then he struck him repeatedly, shifting his target from Vincitor's gut to his face. "I'm going to make you suffer!" He continued to punch. "You're going to pay with your pain!" he shouted with blisteringly red eyes. "Then with your life!"

The villagers fled, but Brac could only focus on his wrath. It was as if he had become a completely different person—nothing could have gotten in the way of his rage. He felt as though he had been put under a spell of inflicting pain and suffering, and Vincitor was the target of all his anguish.

"You little pathetic thrall," was all Vincitor could manage, his words accompanied by a trickle of blood.

"Pathetic, huh?" Brac dropped him and chuckled. "You're the one who's on the ground," he said sadistically, "and now you're about to be in it!" He lifted his foot. For the final crushing blow, he stomped Vincitor's skull multiple times with thoughts of ridding the world of him.

"That's enough!" called a deep voice from behind him. "You've proven your point."

Brac didn't even have to turn around. He knew exactly who it was—he could sense him and recognized that strong, smooth voice. "Lord Bilge, he deserves to—"

"I know how you feel, but he will be taken care of. First, we have to extract Nada from inside of him, then he will be condemned."

Brac turned around with watery eyes. Not only was Bilge standing behind him, but so too were his father and Artiest. "Why?" he asked. "Why didn't you all stop him? I'm talking about the gods. You all are so powerful but refuse to help us humans. Why?"

Bilge stepped up. "We cannot choose saviors. Instead, we have to wait for them to choose themselves. Within every human being is the potential for greatness. You were one we had our eyes on for a very long time. You were quite different at a young age. We knew from how your story was written that you would be one with a great testimony. And with great testimony comes greatness. Look how far you've come, Brac. You have reached a level of power that many will never reach because of fear and doubt. You saved your world by beating the odds. You're a true hero."

Brac's facial expression showed he did not want to hear anything about being a hero that was not going to bring the people he loved back to life. He walked up to Bilge with a blunt look on his face that quickly turned into a wicked facial expression. "You had me fighting all by myself, knowing that you all could have helped me! You could have helped them a long time ago!" he shouted. "And now they're dead!" And he attacked Bilge, swinging a wild left hook at blinding speed.

Bilge blocked the blow without blinking.

Artiest and Brac Guider were speechless.

"You should never lead actions with anger," said Bilge. "You have learned that life holds events that will be incredibly traumatizing. You have to grow strong enough to accept that there will be terrible things, but also accept that you hold the power to stop them as you have done just now. Choosing to put a stop to oppression and to stand up for what's right frees you. You have emancipated yourself from your invisible bondage." He released Brac's hand, and the strangest thing happened. "Look what you've done," said Bilge.

Brac looked up just as the clouds began to disperse. He lifted his hand to shield his eyes from the light pouring through them, then looked around. Grass sprouted, flowers bloomed, trees grew, and fruit ripened, all before his very eyes.

"Brac, look behind you," said Bilge.

His eyes went round in awe as he saw the villagers all streaming back into the village. Then he caught sight of two familiar faces, and tears flowed freely down his cheeks. His mother and Arbre ran toward him, both alive and well again. "Mama, Arbre!" he shouted as they embraced one another with joy. "But I thought—"

"I told you what you have done," said Bilge. "Once you dispersed the negativity that ruled this place, everything began to return to its natural balance."

He had overpowered the negativity that had smothered the world. He was a true hero.

"So, what's next?" Brac asked.

"First, we'll be getting Vincitor out of here, and we'll make sure there aren't any more threats coming to this world anytime soon. We actually have a lot to get done since we have a new savior. Others will come for you because the power you possess spreads throughout the universe, and many are watching. To be completely honest, your whole life is about to change, Brac. You've only made it to the base of the mountain," he said.

Brac knew what it was like to stand at the base of a mountain and at the top of one. There would only be a long, hard climb ahead of him. But he was ready for it.

About the Author

Devis Joseph is a first-time author who briefly studied communications and is largely self-taught along his journey to becoming a novelist. He's from a small town called New Roads, Louisiana, and is here to make an impact on the writing game! He believes to become a writer, you have to "read, read, read, write, write, write," as said by the great Ernest J. Gaines.

www.ingramcontent.com/pod-product-compliance
Lightning Source LLC
Chambersburg PA
CBHW030414310726
48979CB00002B/410